JILL AND MARK

THE 1800S EXPERIMENT

SARAH LAMB

CONTENTS

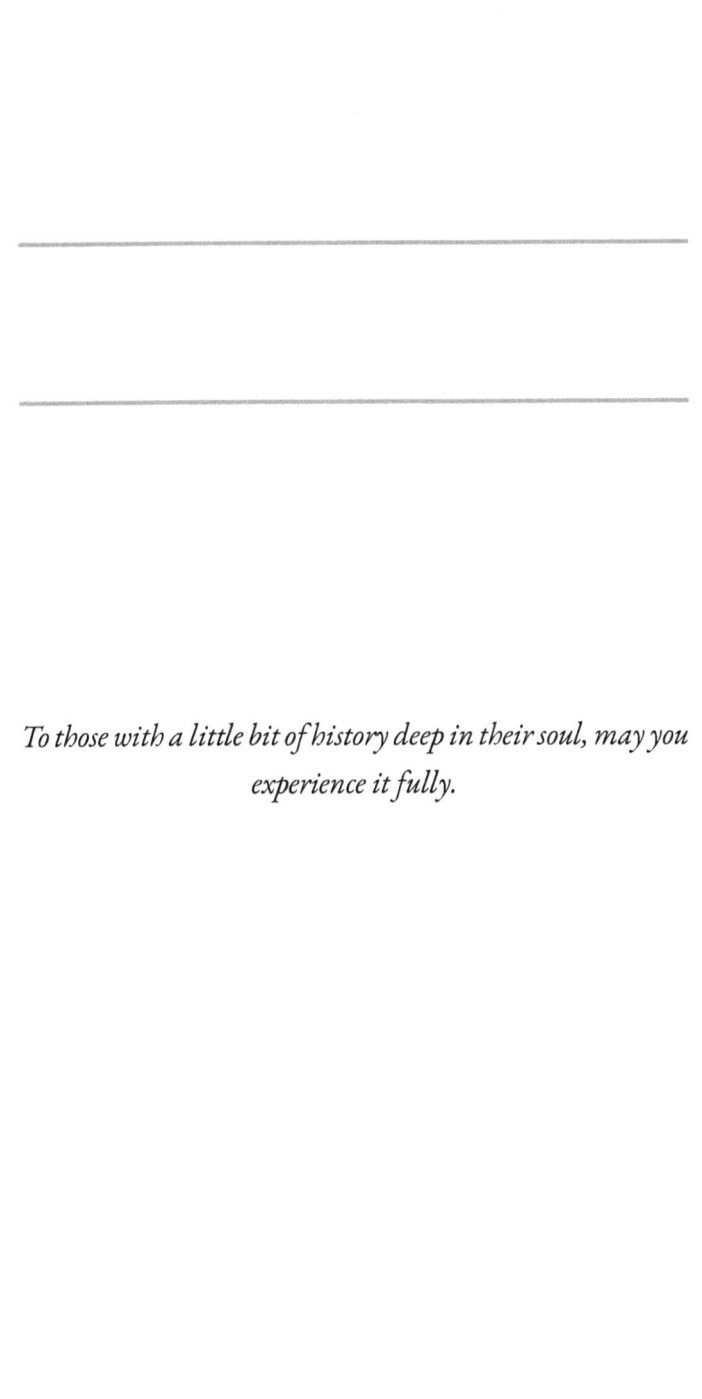

To those with a little bit of history deep in their soul, may you experience it fully.

Chapter 1

Jill didn't even bother to hide her scowl as she balanced two coffee cups in one hand and a box of pastries in the other. The morning had been rough and she doubted it would get any better. She'd spilled the first two cups on her new sweater and had to turn back to the bakery to replace them. Then her skirt had gotten caught in the elevator and torn, and at least a dozen people had laughed at her.

"Here you are," she said, setting the bakery order gingerly on the Your Television Favorites producer's desk.

YTF was a major cable network, and an incredibly popular one. For the last year, she'd been an intern there, doing everything from fetching coffee and dropping off papers from one office to the next, to picking up people from the airport one moment, and lunch orders the next. No two days were the same, which was good.

Sometimes.

The days were always long and she was tired when she went home, but there was always that hope of moving up in the company, and that's what kept her going.

Today had been pretty mundane. Going out to the bakery had been the highlight of her day. Which sounded pretty bad, when she thought about it and her sweater. Thank goodness she had a change of clothes at the office. As she'd changed, she reminded herself she wouldn't be stuck as an intern forever. She was sure of that.

The most interesting thing she'd gotten to do so far in this job was when they were casting for different shows and an extra body was needed here or there to hold a light, spritz on hairspray, or act as an off camera person to feed lines to. She enjoyed that, and liked watching both the screen tests and going over the forms that potential contestants filled out when the opportunity was granted her.

"Thanks, hon," the producer said, taking a sip from his to-go cup and sitting back in his chair. "Sit."

Jill sat, brushing her dark hair out of her face. She didn't like the feeling she was getting. It was radiating in waves that made her feel nervous. It was a little bit "you are in trouble" and "I've got something to tell you." She didn't like either. But especially coming from him. That made it worse. She'd been in that meeting last week when he'd fired three people right after his first sip of coffee.

"Want one?" the producer, Clark Masterson, offered the pastry box.

Jill leaned forward. "Thanks, Dad."

He cleared his throat. "I'm not Dad during the work day," he reminded her.

"Right. Sorry." Jill bit into the cherry Danish and tried to ignore the heat in her cheeks.

Working at YTF was a little bit of a blessing and a curse. With her dad the top producer, at first, many people thought she'd be getting special treatment and good jobs. Luckily for them, though not for her, that couldn't be further from the truth.

Her first month there, she'd been in janitorial. She'd emptied trash cans, scrubbed toilets, vacuumed, and picked up so many gum wrappers that she never wanted to see another stick of Juicy Fruit again. She hadn't complained, though. She knew better. If she did, she might not get to move up for a very long time—if he didn't fire her first.

Thankfully, an intern spot had opened after just a few weeks and she was given it. That's when she moved into fetching. On a slow day, she logged fifteen thousand steps, if that said anything.

But, so far, she'd managed to not step on toes, make a few friends, but most importantly, prove to others that she wasn't there because of who her dad was, but because she'd earned the spot.

And she had. Every day, she worked her hardest. Jill had her eye on a position, and she was going to keep going until she got it.

Her dad set his croissant down and gave a slight frown. That made her worry. Whatever he was going to say couldn't be good. The bite of cherry Danish slid to her stomach and landed like a lump. She reached for her spiced cider to wash it down.

"There's an opportunity. If you want it," he told her.

"What kind?" Jill asked. She'd learned to ask for specifics. After being a yes woman the first few weeks, she'd been taken advantage of, and didn't want to go down that route again. There had been a few unpleasant "opportunities" passed her way. Never again, if she could help it.

"For a show," her father said. He pushed a thick file over to her.

Jill took it, and opened the cover. "*The 1800s Experiment*," she read, then skimmed over the premise. "Huh. A guy, a girl, and the stressors of historical living for four weeks. Will they fall in love or will they become mortal enemies. Sounds a bit...dramatic," Jill said, looking u p.

"That's our business," her father shrugged. "So, you interested?"

"In what way?" Jill took another bite.

"We need two more people there to make it look like the stakes are higher," he answered.

Jill tilted her head. "I don't understand. Why not make it a group then? Get eight or ten people?"

"Viewers are tired of that," her father answered, pushing another paper toward her and tapping his finger on a bar graph. "With endless reality shows for dating or survival, it's gotten a little tiring. This is different. It's one couple—well, two—and living like in the past. We've even found the perfect girl," he said, handing her an application.

"Tara James. Favorite show," Jill read. "*Little House on the Prairie*. Greatest wish, to live like I was in the 1800s." She looked up and laughed. "It's like she was made for this."

"She sort of was," her father agreed. "We were originally casting for *The Moving Maze* or *So You Think You Could be a Doctor,* but when we pitched the idea, our test audiences weren't interested. This one, they were."

"So, who would you pair her up with, if the goal is to see if they fall in love or not?" Jill glanced down at the application again. "You'd want it to be someone she'd have a shot with, not a random stranger, if they're just going to be there four weeks. That's really not a lot of time."

"That's the good part," her father grinned. "She filled out an application with her best friend. Who left some pretty heavy hints that he likes her."

"Let me see. This could be good." Jill snatched the paper her father held out. "Evan Adams. Favorite thing to do. Doesn't matter, as long as I'm with Tara. Favorite thing to eat. Anything Tara makes." She looked up. "You've found your couple alright. Who is the fourth person going to be?"

"I'm not sure yet," her father admitted. "I'm still thinking about it. Are you interested?"

"Maybe," Jill said. "But where would I come into play? If this is to be about them?"

"We don't want this to be too perfect," her father said. "They're going to have a chance at a huge cash prize and, if ratings are high enough, an even larger one. But we don't want it to be too easy. It can't all be sunsets and smiles, and happy music playing in the background. There's no viewership or sponsors with that."

"Soooooo, I'm to...?"

"Shake things up a little. Do your part to help, but stay alert. If things are going too well, put a little drama in. Flirt with the guy. I don't know. Viewers aren't going to know you are a plant until the final interviews."

"It sounds a little weird you telling me to flirt," Jill said, raising a brow. She crossed her arms. "What do I get out of this? As an employee of YTF, I wouldn't be eligible for a prize."

"Not a cash one," her father agreed. He gave her a long look. Fluttering formed in Jill's stomach, and she leaned forward, holding her breath. Here it was. The reason for the strange feeling coming from him.

"There's an opening coming up for an assistant to the casting director," he told her. "It could be yours."

Jill leaned forward, smacked her hands on the desk, then stood up and tucked her dark hair behind her ears. "Well then, you've got yourself a shaker," she said. "They'd better watch out."

"Perfect," her father said. "I knew I could count on you. I'll send the where and when to your email once I have all the details. Now," he said, patting the thick file, "I need you to get this over to Jenkin's office. Tell him to contact the contestants right away."

Taking the thick stack of files with a nod, Jill hurried out. She could hardly believe it. A chance to be a casting assistant. It was a step in the right direction. An opportunity, indeed.

Excitement filled every inch of her. It wasn't until she'd shut the door behind her she realized there was a problem. A big, big problem.

CHAPTER 2

"There's no one else I would rather be with. I'm begging you. Just give me another chance. That's all I'm asking for," Mark pled, feeling a tear form.

There was no answer. He dropped his voice to a whisper, holding one hand out in a desperate gesture. "Please, Rosina. You are all I want. All I think about. We were meant for each other. I...I'd do anything to—"

"Wilson! Boss wants to see you."

Mark Wilson turned with a start from the mirror where he'd been practicing a monologue from the previous day's taping of *Hour by Hour*. It was his dream to be on the show. Word had it a new male character or two would be cast soon, and he planned to audition. Knowing the show as well as he did was hopefully going to be a help. He'd need it too, with as many people as usually turned up for the auditions.

"Thanks, Joe," he said to his fellow medic. "Any idea what it's for?"

"No idea," Joe answered. Then he stopped, putting one hand to his brow dramatically, and grinned, "Maybe he saw your acting just now. Cameras everywhere, right?"

Mark laughed and nodded, then grew a thoughtful look as he glanced around the room. Was Joe right? What if someone *had* noticed him practicing? Maybe he'd get a shot to fulfill his dream. Stranger things had happened.

He turned and picked up the bright red medical supplies backpack he carried everywhere. Though only here for a few months, Mark had enjoyed every minute of his job as set medic. His job encompassed quite a few things, so while most days were luckily injury or accident free, he was always at the ready and never bored. As he left the room, he pondered on how it was surprising that even just on a controlled soap opera set, like *Hour by Hour*, people got injured.

There were several on set medics, and he was the lowest rank of them, in the internal pecking order, but that didn't bother him. His job was mostly the same. He inspected sets to make sure there were no obvious potential hazards, provided medical care when someone had a minor injury, coordinated care for more serious incidents, and was ready at a moment's notice to assist on whatever came up—with a cool head. The last part was important.

It was easy to panic in an emergency, but that could delay the help that the person needed. The radio at his hip crackled and Mark paused his step, then resumed. The call wasn't for him. Good. He didn't want to keep the boss waiting.

He weaved his way down the crowded hallway and through a side corridor, where the offices of the higher ups were. Mark glanced up at the nameplate to make sure he was at the right office and knocked.

"Come in," a voice called.

Mark pushed the door open and entered. He had only been in this office once, the day he interviewed. A little flutter of worry filled his stomach. There wasn't anyone else in here but the boss, no one from casting for *Hour by Hour*. So, why was he here? Was the boss not feeling well?

"Have a seat."

"Thanks, Mr. Masterson," Mark said, as he sat, lowering his medical backpack to his feet. "Joe told me you wanted to see me?"

"I do." The producer laced his hands and set them on the desk before him. "I wanted to offer an opportunity."

An opportunity? Was this it? An audition for *Hour by Hour*? Mark nodded, tried to put what he hoped was a nonchalant expression on his face, and smiled. "Sure, I'm all ears."

"We've got a new reality show we're finishing the casting on, and finalizing the set," Mr. Masterson said.

"Okay. Need me to look over the set?" Mark asked.

"No. I need a fourth person, a male, to act as though he's one of the contestants." The producer leaned back in his chair. "You're a medic, which would also be important, as this is a reality show where there won't be cameras following the contestants. There will be static cameras throughout, there to simply observe them."

"So, no crew on site?" Mark asked. That was unusual.

"None. Except for you and one other. She'll also be acting as though she's one of the contestants."

"What's her job?" Mark asked.

The producer smiled. "To make sure things don't stay too calm and go too well over those four weeks."

Mark tapped his fingers on his knee and tried not to feel disappointed. He'd let himself get his hopes up that he'd be offered the chance to be on a real show. Not some reality thing where the characters were forgotten the minute the TV clicked off.

"One more thing. The show is to be set as though it were the 1800s. As usual, there are prizes. This time, we're giving the contestants a wad of cash if they survive living as though it's back then. Since you'd be ineligible for a monetary prize," the producer continued, "I'd like to offer you something else instead. It's only fair. Of course, you'll get your regular pay too, since you'll be working for the company. The other two contestants won't know that."

Mark sat up. "Oh really? What would I be offered?" he asked.

"A golden ticket," Mr. Masterson said. He studied Mark for a moment. "I know you'd like to act. *Hour by Hour* will be running auditions in eight weeks for three new roles, two of them male."

Mark held his breath and swallowed hard. "Is that so?" he said, hoping he didn't sound too eager.

"I'll get you the audition," the producer continued, "and promise you pushed through to the second round. The rest is up to you and your acting abilities."

His heart hammering, Mark nodded. "I'm in," he said. Getting to the second round was huge. There would be likely hundreds of people trying out for the parts. Maybe thousands if it was an open call. Only a dozen or two made it to the second round.

"Good. I'll send over the details soon," Mr. Masterson said. "One more thing."

"What's that?" Mark asked. He hoped it wouldn't be a dealbreaker. He'd already agreed.

The producer hesitated. "The other contestant, the employee here..." He was quiet a moment, "Keep her safe."

That wasn't what he'd expected. Mark nodded. "I'll do my best."

"That's all I ask. Thank you for your time."

Dismissed, Mark nodded, and stood, still feeling a little in shock. Stardom might be just around the corner.

He headed toward the breakroom. His lunch had just started and he looked forward to a few minutes to digest the news.

Someone else was already there, sitting in one of the hard plastic chairs, scrolling on her phone. She looked up. "Hey."

"Hey." Mark grabbed a sandwich and a soda from the machine, and looked at her. "Aren't you the head producer's daughter?"

"Yep," she answered, not looking up. "Jill."

He sat down a few seats away and unwrapped the sandwich. Neither of them spoke. Finally, he asked, "You know anything about that show that's being filmed as though it's the 1800s?"

She looked up at him. "I'm supposed to be there with the contestants. I don't know much about it really."

"Oh. So you're supposed to be the troublemaker," he said.

She tensed and then glared at him. "Doing my job, you mean? As the producer's daughter, you don't get to say no very much if you want to keep your job and not be accused of nepotism."

"You're right. Sorry," Mark said. "I'm Mark. I'll be there with you, your sidekick and medic on call." He decided not to add in the part that her dad had asked him to keep her safe. He didn't think she'd like that.

She looked at him carefully. "Oh, okay." She shrugged. "No idea what we're doing or what it will be like. I'm reading up on the time period now."

"Great. If you learn anything good, fill me in. I got zero information," Mark said. "No idea what to expect."

"What did you get offered?" she asked. "I assume it was something."

"A free pass to the second round of auditions for *Hour by Hour*." He didn't miss her smirk. "What about you?"

"An interview to be a casting assistant," she said. "So, I'll be doing my best. I really want that spot."

"So do I," Mark said. "It's sure going to be interesting doing this."

"Awful, you mean," Jill corrected. "Do you know how much physical labor will be involved? Did you know they didn't have toilets back then? No plumbing whatsoever. The beds are usually filled with straw and bugs are everywhere."

"That's...worrying," Mark said, finishing his soda.

"I'm not done," Jill said. "We'll have to take care of livestock, can't have real showers or baths, while sweating ourselves silly, and have to learn to cook over a fire for all of our meals." She made a face. "Wish I could have said no, but like I said, when you do, people think you are calling in favors. I'd rather have my shot at the job than not, though.

So, 1800s, here I come!" She made a sarcastic gesture of one finger making tiny circles in the air.

"I get that. Never been in your spot before, but I understand. It'll be fine. I doubt it will be as bad as you are thinking. After all, this is reality TV and your dad is the head producer. You really think he'd let you suffer?"

"Knowing Dad? For ratings? Yes." Jill looked back down at her phone. "I've never even been camping, so I am a little worried."

Mark gave her a grin. "It's going to be fine. For myself, I'm going to focus on doing what I have to do, get through those weeks, and use the free time practicing my lines for that audition. I bet those physical chores will help me gain a little muscle for the role too."

"Do you think we'll get much free time?" Jill asked. "With just four of us, I'm worried we'll be slaving away all day."

"Nah. It's going to be easy," Mark assured her. "Piece of cake."

A few weeks later, those words would replay through his mind and he'd regret every syllable.

CHAPTER 3

Jill scowled and pulled the scratchy blanket higher. It was only the first night and she couldn't leave fast enough. The day had started off okay. First, there had been a meeting explaining what was going to happen. She and the two contestants had said hello, all decked out in their old-fashioned clothes, listened to an overview of what to expect, and were off to the 1800s site.

Jill couldn't remember how many acres the place was, but it was far too many for her liking. The place was huge, much bigger than she thought it would be, and the list of chores they'd been given felt ten times as long.

As to be expected, the girls had all the domestic chores but several outside ones as well. How she was going to survive was beyond her. Jill was not outdoorsy in the least. The first time she'd had to use the outhouse terrified her and she vowed to go as little as possible. Evidently, critters and creatures would find the space and start filling it. At least they'd been warned. She didn't want to sit and get bitten.

The very thought made her shudder. And more than terrified her.

Jill let her eyes roam. The layout of the house was okay, she guessed. She and Tara, the other girl, got the larger cabin. They had two small beds opposite of each other and set to the side. Each of them had a large wooden trunk to store their items in. Clothes were hung on pegs.

There was a kitchen with the stove and a table. Shelves lined the walls to hold the dishes. So far, everything was overall going well, she had to admit. Except for the fact there was going to be a lot of work to do.

She wasn't looking forward to any of it. Right now, she really missed her bed. Cotton sheets. Running water. A toilet. Iced tea.

Jill sighed and closed her eyes. *The sooner I fall asleep, the sooner I get to tomorrow and it's one day less here and one day closer to casting assistant. I never thought a single day could feel so long.*

Across the way, Tara slept peacefully. She would. Jill wasn't sure if she liked Tara. She was too cheerful. Too happy to be there. It was almost going to be fun to throw a little conflict and drama this way and that. Maybe wipe that smile off Tara's perfect face.

So far, she'd been nice. Played it safe. It was only a matter of time though. It was important to let Tara and Evan settle in. Once they had, she'd strike. How, Jill wasn't sure.

As she tried to fall asleep in the uncomfortable bed, she also wondered. If this season did good, could there be a season two? What would it need? She decided to make notes and then plan it all out. Maybe that would win her the casting assistant spot.

Eventually, Jill's eyes grew heavy, and she'd hardly closed them before a loud crash woke her.

"Oops! Sorry!" Tara giggled. "I dropped the kettle. It was heavier than I thought it would be."

Jill groaned and rolled over. "Could you be quieter? I'm trying to sleep."

"Oh no," Tara said. "You've got to get up. That's the rule. Everyone wakes at six." She came over to Jill and looked at her seriously. "I won't let you throw away your shot at the prize by sleeping in."

That got her moving. Jill jumped up. She got dressed and poked at the bread dough they'd set to rise the night before. It actually didn't look bad.

Jill glanced at Tara, who was humming as she mixed dry oats with steaming water. A tiny flicker of guilt flashed through her. Tara had been worried about her being sent home without a prize. She had no idea that couldn't happen. Jill bit her lip. She hoped Tara wouldn't be too nice to her. That would make it hard for her to stir things up.

The last thing she wanted was any sort of guilt. She was here for one reason, and one reason only. To get that assistant spot.

No matter what she had to do for it.

"So, how do we get the guys over for breakfast?" Tara asked.

"I don't know. Is there like, a bell or something?" Jill answered. "Or we could just walk over. No rule about that, right?"

"I don't think there is," Tara said with a grimace. "I just don't want to be kicked off the show. Not the first day."

Jill rolled her eyes. "Whatever. It's fine. They aren't kicking anyone off. It's if you quit. We'll go together. That way, we are each other's chaperone."

"That's a perfect idea!" Tara said, in that cheerful tone Jill knew she was going to get sick of.

They hurried across the short distance to the guy's place. Jill raised her skirt a little to avoid the mud. The cleaner she stayed, the easier to do laundry. She couldn't remember the last time she'd worn a dress, but here she was.

Pale pink flowers splattered all over the fabric. A pink ribbon at the sleeves sewn into a little bow kept tickling her whenever she pushed her hair out of her eyes. Whoever had chosen this from costuming was going to get an earful when she got back. Her other two dresses were just as awful. Tara at least got one in checks and one plain one. Hers were all flowers. Someone must dislike her.

The feeling was mutual.

Jill couldn't help but scowl. She was pretty sure at this point her face was going to be stuck that way. This place stunk—literally—and she was ready to go home.

"Hey, girls," Mark said as he leaned in the doorway.

Jill felt her cheeks color, though she didn't know why. He winked at them, and Tara just laughed. How was she always so calm?

"Hey! Breakfast is ready." Tara pointed to their cabin.

"On our way," Evan called, coming through the door.

Jill simply turned and walked back toward the house. She felt oddly awkward right now and wasn't sure why.

Over oatmeal with only a light drizzle of honey to sweeten it, they discussed the plan for the day. Jill listened carefully. She'd decided the first day not to stir up too much drama, but you never knew when something said might come in handy later. She'd been given a list of things to listen out for, and suggestions on how to ramp up tension and strike at emotional vulnerabilities.

"Do we want to just work together doing everything? One chore at a time?" Evan asked.

"We can't," Tara told him, shaking her head. "There are ones that women have to do that the men didn't back then, and vice versa."

"That means those barn animals are ours," Mark sighed. He glanced toward the barn. "Darn. If there weren't cameras, I'd offer to trade. I'm a great chef."

"It's fine! It's only for a few weeks," Tara said, standing up from the table and grabbing the dishes. "It's all good. We've got this!"

"Right," Evan agreed.

Jill didn't feel so confident about that, but didn't say anything.

As the guys left to attend to the animals, Jill helped Tara wash the dishes. They heated water in the kettle, then shaved off a piece from a large block of soap. There was a second bucket with clean water to rinse that Jill had fetched.

They'd been reminded to use the dishwater on the garden somewhere, and the rinse water for washing up later. Water was difficult to get at times and none of it could be wasted. A far contrast from when you'd leave the water running in the tap to wash your hands or a frying pan at home.

Jill wondered how long it would take to get used to that. At least when she got home, maybe she'd have built the habit of wasting less water.

"So, tell me all about you and Evan," Jill urged, looking over.

Time to get to work.

Tara blushed. She looked so cute it almost irritated Jill. No wonder Evan liked her.

"There's not a lot to tell," Tara said, plunging her hands into the soapy water.

"We've known each other for a while."

"Keep talking," Jill said. "How long have you been dating?"

"Oh! We aren't," Tara said, then she blushed even deeper. "At least...not as much more than friends." Her eyes dropped, and Jill wondered if that was a flash of sadness.

"Oh. You guys seemed like a couple," Jill said, thinking back to Evan's form he'd filled out for the show. He'd practically seemed to worship her.

"We've never been serious," Tara said. "Though I wish..." She shook her head and scrubbed furiously at a plate. "Never mind."

"You wish he'd be more serious?" Jill pressed. How was she to cause drama with the boyfriend if he wasn't a boyfriend? Tara wasn't making this easy.

"Yeah. I do. I think he'd like to be, but Evan's a little shy at times." Tara pressed her lips together. "I'll be honest. That does annoy me."

"Maybe he just needs a little push into it," Jill shrugged, wiping one of the plates dry. She set it on top of another plate that had already been washed.

"Maybe," Tara agreed. "I won't lie, I'm hoping this is a chance for us to take things to the next level. Admittedly, I didn't realize how little we'd likely see of each other. Maybe we'd have backed out if we'd known."

"We've only just gotten here. There's time," Jill assured her. She walked toward the house with the plates and smiled to herself as she reached for her hidden notebook and opened it to a fresh page.

Ensure coupledom.

Shy.

Too sweet. Ugh.

Get it done = Assistant spot.

Tara walked in. "What are you doing?" she asked.

"Nothing," Jill answered, sliding the notebook into her pocket.

"Okay," Tara answered, in a tone that sounded like she knew Jill was up to something. She strode over to the list. "We've got wool to card, the garden to tend to, and eggs to collect from the chickens."

"Ugh. Chickens first," Jill grumbled. "Let's get it out of the way."

She followed Tara outside to the small chicken house behind the barn. There, for the next half hour, she and Tara shrieked and ran from angry chickens that pecked, flapped their wings, and fluttered wildly at them.

Their result was four broken eggs, three cracked, and one unblemished.

"An improvement from yesterday," Tara said shakily as they walked away, her bright smile temporarily dimmed.

"Stupid chickens," Jill muttered.

"We need them," Tara said simply.

Jill couldn't argue with that. Not out loud anyway. She was counting down the days, though. And might never look at a chicken the same ever again. At first, she'd thought them pretty things, walking around and pecking at the dirt with their glossy feathers catching the sun.

Not anymore.

Her opinion now was severely different. And not one for polite company.

A shout from the barn caught her attention, and Tara winced. "I bet Evan's having trouble with the cow again," she said as she opened the garden gate.

"At least I'm not the only one struggling," Jill muttered under her breath.

Jill followed Tara into the garden and shut the gate behind her. For the next hour, she pulled weeds and wiped her sleeve across her sweaty forehead and complained.

Tara made it all feel so much worse. Miss Mary Sunshine. She was humming and smiling. She looked sweaty too, but somehow she also looked adorable. It made Jill even more upset.

She couldn't wait to go back home, have a shower, an icy drink, and—

"Hey girls."

Jill glanced up. Mark stood there and grinned at them, Evan at his elbow. Her face warmed, and Jill hoped they thought it was just the heat pelting down on them.

"How's it going?" Tara asked.

"That cow," Evan growled. "She's going to be steaks soon. Just watch."

"Don't you dare," Tara scolded, shaking her finger at him. "She's our butter and milk."

"She's also the source of the bruise I can't show you," he said, pointing to his rear.

Mark laughed. "Sure does have it in for him." He looked at her. "Everything going well over here?"

"Sure is," Jill said.

That wasn't what she wanted to say. She wanted to tell him how much she hated the place. To have someone to commiserate with. Mark knew she was a plant, and knew why she was here. Even if he didn't feel the same and couldn't do anything to make things better, at least if she could gripe to him, just have a mutual understanding about why she was doing this, maybe she'd feel better.

Just like Tara and Evan though, she and Mark couldn't spend much time together. Not by themselves.

A loud cracking in the sky startled everyone, and huge fat raindrops pelted.

"See you later," Mark called, as he and Evan waved and jogged to their house.

Jill ran into the girls' cabin and set the eggs on the counter. Tara followed close behind and shut the door.

"Isn't the rain so pretty?" she asked looking through the window. "Look at how helpfully it's watering the garden. That means we don't have to do it later."

"Yes," Jill grit out. She mentally counted, then winced. There were too many days left. If Tara kept being this cheerful, they'd feel even longer.

Oh, she was glad they wouldn't have to haul heavy buckets of water to the garden, but did Tara ever complain or get upset? Ever?

Tara chattered away as she cleaned up and changed her dress. Jill tuned her out as best as she could. Tara continued to talk nonstop while they took turns churning butter, each of them switching when their arms started to ache.

Jill nodded here and there, answered questions and asked a few, but her mind was focused on one thing. The future.

The weight of the notebook in her pocket grounded her. It was a sign that she wasn't stuck here with little Miss Happy, that she wasn't stuck here outdoors. She was biding her time.

Time that couldn't pass too quickly.

CHAPTER 4

Mark woke and stretched. Used to getting up early, the hours didn't bother him. While he was more tired than usual from all the hard work, it simply meant he fell asleep faster and slept well.

Evidently, the same couldn't be said for Evan, who tossed and turned. Mark wished he had headphones to drown him out. But, having grown up with a little brother who snored like a freight train, he was pretty good at ignoring it.

The first few days had been fine. That's about it, though. Fine. He'd hoped things would go better, be easier as time went on, but that wasn't the case.

The chores in themselves weren't that hard, but they were physically demanding. He and Evan had been tasked with sawing down small trees to make another outbuilding. They would fell the trees, strip the branches, then Lincoln Log them into a building. At least, that's how it sounded on the list they were given.

As the sun rose, Mark slipped outside for a few moments alone. When he'd first been offered the job, he thought he'd have a lot more free time. Living the simple life, wasn't that what folks did? They gathered around a fire in the evening, read, played games, sewed, whatever.

The reality was far different. When they weren't too tired to talk, it was usually a discussion of what needed to be done next on their list.

Mark felt for the packet of papers he'd snuck in with him. It was a script for an episode of *Hour by Hour*. He'd hardly had any time to practice his lines. Either someone was always around or else he was simply too exhausted.

The only good thing about all of this was that he'd be leaving soon. Back to a real bed and a shower. There was a lake they could bathe in, however, the possibility of catching something like a flesh eating disease was a little too much of a worry for him to let himself do that. So, he hauled water from the well, heated it, and had as good of a wash as he could manage.

Luckily, the clothes weren't too bad. They honestly weren't too different from what he usually wore. Long sleeve button up and pants. The girls, they had it worse. Those long dresses. He knew Jill wished she could trade, but it wasn't allowed. He felt bad for her each time her long skirt got tangled on something or she tripped.

Mark hurried into the barn. He'd been so lost in his thoughts, he'd forgotten the others would be waking up soon. He didn't want to miss his chance to practice.

Walking inside, he glanced around, choosing a spot to stand where he'd be able to see if anyone approached. It was also near a camera, so the folks back home could see how serious he was about the part. He knew this cut wouldn't make it online, so no harm in being seen. He took the script out, looked at it for a moment, then readied himself.

"Carissa, darling, my life is yours. If we never escape from this deserted island, I want you to know one thing..."

Mark paused, with what he hoped was the right amount of drama, and gazed into the distance, then back at the cow, putting as much smolder into his face as he could.

"That night, when you walked in on me and your sister's cousin's neighbor's niece's friend...nothing had happened. She merely had something in her eye. Being a former child prodigy airline pilot turned surgeon, I felt it my duty to assist."

Mark tossed his hair, then struck a pose Leonardo, the character he was reading, would do. "The entire time I was saving her cornea, with only a paintbrush and a paperclip—"

"What?" Mark interrupted himself. "That's impossible." He frowned and scanned the script again. "That can't be right. Who wrote this? Are they for real?"

He heard a giggle, and looked up to see Jill. "I can't believe you want to be on that corny show," she scoffed.

"Most episodes aren't too bad," Mark said defensively. "I think I'm just being given the challenging lines to see if I can pull them off."

She laughed again and waved a hand. "You can. I'm sure of it." Then she started to pace. "Oh my gosh, I can't stand much more of this. I came out here to try and regain my sanity."

Mark tucked his script back into his shirt. "Hang in there. Remember... a chance at the job you want."

"Yeah. I know. And I'm sure it's worth it. Just..." Jill closed her eyes. "She's driving me crazy. You know, Tara is nice. She really is. But she's also so darn cheerful and happy all the time. This—" she waved her arm around the barn, then gestured wildly—"this is not my happy place." She took a deep breath, obviously trying to calm down.

"I understand." Mark shook his head. "It's Tara, Tara, Tara in our place. And snoring. Evan snores. Like, walls shaking, roof falling in kind of loud. I had to grow up with a brother who did. It's been nice not having that again. Tara's in for a surprise, if she doesn't already know."

Jill laughed. She looked pretty when she smiled. He hadn't seen too much of that, but seeing her eyes filled with a hint of mirth, combined with the way her face lit up, made his heart suddenly race. He liked seeing her happy. She was always so serious. This smile suited her.

"You get me. I'm glad," she said. Jill took a peek around the corner to check the cabins. Houses. Whatever. Mark wasn't sure what to call them. He honestly didn't care. He was just doing his job. Jill looked back at him. "Anyway. I wanted to see you."

"I'm right here," Mark said, waving at himself. Her cheeks pinked again and he grinned. She sure blushed easy. "What's up?"

"It's time to ramp things up," Jill said, now looking serious. "Nothing seems to phase them. Not when I let the chickens loose, not when her clean laundry "accidently" blew away. None of the little stuff I've done has ruffled Tara or Evan. Things are going too well for them right now and they are really embracing this historical living. It's like they were made for it. Today is a perfect day to do things differently. It looks like their relationship is moving forward, so it's time for me to do what Dad asked. There's really not a lot of time left to be here."

"Thank goodness for that. Go on," Mark said.

"Tara told me she thinks Evan is going to try and talk to her today about taking a step forward with their relationship."

"So, what am I supposed to do?" Mark asked. He glanced toward the small cabin where Evan was. "Speaking of Evan, I better head back soon. He's going to wake up when that cow starts calling for him. He startles every time."

"Better him or you than me. That thing is a fly magnet. We can walk and talk," Jill said. "I just need a little help. Here. This is for you." She handed him a book.

Mark took it, slowly walking toward the cabin. "What's this?"

Jill smirked. "*This* is hope. You're going to give it, and then yank it away. It's got to work. I'm running low on options."

"I'm not following." Mark looked between her and the book, then opened to a random page. He started flipping through. "It's full of how to's. How to skin a hog. How to grow beans. How to tell if your horse is sick or lazy."

Jill huffed out a breath. "This book has lots of rules in it too. Especially about dating. Well, they called it courting. Whatever. You are going to set it out. Let him see it's possible to start a relationship. That he could do so safely, now and here, instead of waiting to go back home. Then hide the book."

"Hide it?" Mark furrowed his brow. "But then, how will he be able to do the stuff it says he can do?"

"That's just it. It will throw him off balance. I think it's unlikely he'll be able to do more than glance at it before it's gone. Remember, we aren't here to help their romance. We are supposed to just see if it can survive."

"If you say so," Mark said doubtfully. "But what about you? I'm just the sidekick, remember? Wasn't this supposed to be your job?" He held the book up.

"I'll flirt with Evan," Jill answered.

It was Mark's turn to smirk. "Oh? Is that what you wanted all along?" He laughed as Jill's face turned flame red.

"He's not my type," she protested, "and it's not something I'm keen on, but it's a surefire way to get them to argue. Ratings, remember?"

"Ratings is your department," Mark said, stopping in front of the door. "Backup and medical emergencies were my job." He opened the door and walked part way inside.

Jill whispered, "So? You'll do it?"

"Yep," Mark replied in his own whisper. "I want the audition as much as you want your interview." Jill turned to go, but he said, "Hey."

She spun back to face him. "Yeah?"

Mark's mouth suddenly went dry, but before he could stop himself, the words flew out of his mouth. "So, what is your type?"

There was a sound behind him and he quickly shut the door before he could hear her answer. Through the window, he could see Jill running toward the girl's house. He watched her slip inside then stifled a sigh. What was wrong with him? Was he...flirting with her?

He shook that thought away. No. He was curious. That was all. Trying to get to know her.

Time for business. The real reason he was there. Being pushed to the second round of the audition.

"Morning, sleeping beauty," he laughed, as he turned to face Evan.

Evan's hair was sticking up in a dozen different directions. He also looked like he hadn't even slept. Mark wondered why that was. The beds? They weren't the best, but with all their work, he could sleep on the floor no problem.

Maybe it was just being in a new place? Then it hit him. Jill had said he might be talking to Tara today. Maybe he'd had trouble falling asleep, wondering how to take their relationship to the next level. He grinned. Time to do his part.

When Tara came to the door a moment later to tell them breakfast was ready, he eased the book Jill had given him onto the table, and walked away. Would Evan see it?

It took all he had not to gloat or punch the air in excitement when Evan walked over to the book and asked about it. Jill sure could call things. She'd be perfect in casting. If she got a job there, did that mean he'd seen her more? He wasn't really sure how often casting assistants were on set where the medics were.

Then he wondered why that even came to him. This was work. Anyway, Jill was the boss's daughter. Off limits. His job was to keep her safe. Not date her.

Evan flipped through the book a moment, talking excitedly. Mark just nodded, not paying him a bit of attention. Though he became alert when Evan put it back on the table. Just as they were walking out the door, Mark made sure Evan didn't see, and slid the small book into his pocket. He'd hide it later in the barn. There was a special box in there that only he knew about. It would be the perfect location.

He suspected Jill was right about hiding the book too. Knowing Evan, he would go crazy looking for it. The short glimpse he'd had at the section for the rules of courtship would make him curious to see just how much he and Tara could do within the rules.

Too bad he wouldn't be able to do that now. Mark refused to let himself feel guilty. There was something big at stake.

Evan and Tara knew it too. They had been very careful to follow every rule. To be fair, Mark and Jill also had. They just didn't have the same prize waiting for them. Whereas Evan and Tara had a chance at a lot of money, for Mark it was his future on the line, and he was going to do whatever it took to get that audition.

CHAPTER 5

Jill felt guilty as she watched Tara and Evan laugh as they hung out the laundry together. It was a disgusting feeling that filled her with self loathing. Mark had told her all had gone well with showing the book then hiding it. That part of the plan had worked. She hoped, anyway.

Used to doing things herself, it was hard to trust someone else to be her partner. She wanted to see for herself the book was gone.

Over lunch, she'd batted her eyes at Evan, brushed her hand against his, did all those little things to let him know she was interested in him. She couldn't tell if he'd noticed, but Tara did. Mark had as well.

Tara's face had been one of anger. She hadn't spoken, but Jill could tell she wasn't a happy pioneer. Mark had studied her carefully. Was he analyzing her for audition fodder? She wasn't sure.

The flirting hadn't gone the best, but Jill planned to try it again. With practice, she'd improve.

But would that ruin any potential chance she had with Mark? She hoped not.

And why would she even think that? She and Mark weren't anything. Not even friends. No, she was just doing her job.

She was trying very hard to stir up a little something for the viewers. And her father. And every one of them she did made her feel sick. She didn't have a boyfriend, and so she had never experienced someone making a pass at him, but if she did, she'd hate that girl right now for interrupting, and flirting, and making life difficult.

It was amazing, honestly, that Tara hadn't gotten upset at her, though the small flashes of confusion or hurt she saw flicker in the other girl's eyes now and again made her feel really crummy. Hurting Tara wasn't something she wanted to do.

Business was business, but when the other person didn't know that, it made it feel personal.

Jill also couldn't help but worry about the audience response. Oh, she knew that there always had to be that mean girl, and she was cast in that role. But how much editing would be done? Would they make her look worse than she was?

The days were passing by too slowly. It didn't help Jill felt a little left out. Lonely.

Only a short distance away, Tara's laughter carried to her ears. Evan was making a funny face, and Tara was chasing him, smacking at him with a wet sock. They looked so perfect together. So natural. Like they'd known each other for forever, and were already a couple. Even if they weren't, or never became one, it was obvious the two of them were the best of friends and would be that way forever.

Jill was a little jealous that Tara had a friend to be doing this challenge with. She didn't have one. It would be nice to have someone to play around with, talk to, someone who knew her and understood her.

Okay, yes, Mark was there, but he wasn't really a friend. He wasn't quite even a coworker, someone she saw on a regular basis and could at least fake some friendly conversation with. Though they worked for the same place, she'd never met him until recently, so it wasn't the same thing at all like Tara and Evan had, knowing each other for years and having easy conversations.

When they spoke, it wasn't ever for too long. She guessed it wasn't difficult, exactly, to talk to him, but it wasn't overly friendly either. Their conversations had mostly been about the show, very little about themselves.

That said... there had been a few times her tongue hadn't seemed to want to work when a personal question had come up.

Like when he asked her what her type was.

Even thinking about it right now made Jill blush. Why had he asked her that? And, more importantly, why hadn't she minded? She'd wanted to answer, to say tall, dark, handsome, want-to-be actor types to tease him, but the words had frozen in her brain and her tongue. Maybe because they wouldn't have been a tease. They'd have been the truth.

Evan had woken up then, interrupting them, and her next thought was rushing back so he wouldn't see her and Tara wouldn't be suspicious about anything she was doing.

She let her eyes drift off in the distance where Tara and Evan were nearly done with the laundry, then she looked at where she'd last seen Mark. A moment later, she spotted him. Mark was doing pushups. It was hard not to roll her eyes. And feel annoyed. Here she was, washing dishes, kneading bread dough, always cleaning and fixing and doing, and he had time to goof off? Why couldn't she?

Earlier, he'd been in the barn, practicing his lines for *Hour by Hour*. After lunch, he'd vanished to work out. Was he even taking this seriously?

Actually...

Jill glanced around. No one was nearby. Not close enough to notice what she was doing, anyway. That meant no one would notice if she stopped working for a few moments to write in her notebook while her thoughts were still fresh.

She snuck inside, pulled the notebook and pen from her secret spot under her mattress, and opened it.

Jill gave a careful look over what she'd already written, then jotted down more notes. Her head was bent low. The notebook was small, too small, but it was a reminder of what would be.

Even if she didn't get the assistant job, at least she'd be back as intern with the chance at moving up in the company.

She tapped her pen against the notebook and let her eyes drift toward Mark again. Would they run into each other once they went home? Maybe at work? Hang out sometime?

A thing like this supposedly changed people. The two of them could talk about it. Reminisce. It would be nice. Friends weren't something she had a lot of. Okay. Any of. For one, there just wasn't time, not if she wanted to get the job of her dreams. For another, well, sometimes it was hard to know who wanted to be your friend because of who you were, versus because your dad had a thick wallet.

Hah. If only those people realized she'd had to earn everything she got. It wasn't given. Still, that didn't stop people from trying to be friendly, thinking she could get them a spot at the company, an audition, whatever.

Jill sighed. What she wouldn't give to be Tara. Who obviously had it all together, and then some. Her life must be so perfect.

Which was why it was her job to mess it up some. Not too much, not so much that it would upset her or get her hurt or totally ruin her relationship, but just enough that Jill would be able to do what she needed to do to make sure that *her* future was just as put together and perfect.

In casting.

Of course, she had no illusions that it would be easy being an assistant to a casting director. Assistant was a step up from intern, to be sure. However, it was also going to be long hours, hard work, and coffee runs—much like now. The difference was, she'd be invited to meetings, auditions, and planning periods, getting an inside look at how things were done.

The idea filled her with a fresh energy, and Jill hunched over her notebook. She'd not only finish these four weeks she'd been assigned, she'd go back with enough ideas to knock the socks off of her dad and the casting director she'd interview with.

About fifteen minutes later, Jill stood. She checked on the bread dough that was rising and then peered at the stovetop. Should she stir the stew? It was strange letting something sit all day on the stove, but that's how they had to cook.

Cooking wasn't something Jill was very good at, but surely she could stir without too much trouble. She lifted the heavy ladle, gave a few halfhearted swirls in the soup, and watched as chunks of potatoes rose to the top, only to fall again.

Where was everyone? It had gotten really quiet. Too quiet.

Jill stepped to the front of the cabin. Mark wasn't by the barn anymore. Maybe he'd gone inside it, or back to his own place for a nap?

Tara and Evan must still be on their walk. Had he asked her to be more serious? Had he noticed the book was missing yet? She didn't think so, but it would be hard to keep a straight face. That's why she was glad she didn't know what Mark had done with it. Then she wouldn't have to lie.

Yawning, Jill glanced up. It had gotten a little dark. The clouds were thicker. It looked like it might rain again. Just what she wanted. More time stuck indoors.

I guess it just adds to the authentic experience.

Jill decided to go look for Mark to make sure he'd hidden the book, when the sound of a bloodcurdling scream filled the air.

CHAPTER 6

"It's mine!" Mark hissed, his fingers curled into a fist. "I fought six lions for it. I braved a herd of wild rhinos. I rode across four hundred miles of sandstorms to get this. I—"

A scream, one that could only be described as ear splitting and filled with terror, pulled Mark from his practice lines.

He set off at a run toward the sound. Jill was right next to him. He saw Tara, seemingly frozen to a spot while Evan was holding a large stick. Mark looked around for something to help defend the girls with, but there wasn't anything.

With a burst of speed, he pulled ahead, putting himself between whatever the danger was and Jill.

When Evan pulled out a kitten from a large bush, setting everyone's minds at ease, Mark nearly collapsed. The girls, seemingly unconcerned that just a moment before panic had been filling the air, were all coos and giggles and baby talk as they swooped in on the ball of white fluff.

When Tara proclaimed it hers, naming it Snowball, Mark didn't miss the flash of sadness in Jill's eyes. He'd have to ask her about that later. The expression was more than just disappointment at not finding it first. He could see a story there.

He watched as Tara took the kitten to the girl's cabin. Jill stayed a few steps behind. When he looked over, she had her hand on Evan's arm and was giving him a smile. One that made him feel jealous. He didn't quite know why.

Yeah, he knew what she was doing. Knew it wasn't real. Heck, they hardly knew each other, but the smile she was giving him, that wink, was one he wished she'd give him.

Evan and Tara returned to their walk, and he caught up to Jill, who was hunched over at the outdoor table. Her head was lowered, but when he got close enough, he was able to see she looked miserable.

"You okay?" he asked her. She was acting strange. A stark contrast to how she'd been a few moments ago. Then, she'd been smiling and giggly. Now she was quiet and looked like she might cry.

"Just hate this," she said. "I feel like a fraud. I stink at flirting. This whole thing feels so awkward. How does Tara not hate me already?"

He sat next to her. For some reason he couldn't explain, Mark put his arm around her shoulders. "You're pretty good at the flirting," he told her. "It looked real to me."

"Honestly?" She looked up at him.

Reluctantly, he dropped his arm. 1800s. No real physical contact. "Yep. I mean, almost made me jealous."

Her cheeks went pink. "Really?" she asked.

"Tell me about the kitten," Mark said, nodding toward the cabin.

"Snowball?" Jill looked in confusion toward the cabin.

"I guess. It's just..." he thought for a moment. He wasn't sure he wanted to say it, then shrugged. "You looked really sad for a moment when Tara said it was hers now."

Jill let out a bitter laugh. "Yeah. I guess I am. Jealous too. It's like she gets it all. The kitten. A boyfriend. A friend. The perfect life. I've got none of that."

"I guess I don't know too much about you," Mark said. "So, no friends? No boyfriend? I find that hard to believe."

"I'm always too busy working. You know how it is." She was looking in her lap though, and he wasn't quite sure if that was the whole truth. Jill glanced at him, then looked away. "Sometimes it's also hard to tell if people like you for who you are, or what they think your dad can do for them."

"That makes a lot of sense. But in a way, it surprises me about you being so busy and working all the time. I didn't realize that you were so career driven."

Jill laughed. Another of those pained, humorless sounds. "I bet I seem like the type of girl who has stuff given to her and doesn't have to work for it. Nothing could be further from the truth. My dad makes me work hard. Everything I have I work for."

Mark wanted to put his arm around her again. He knew he wasn't allowed to. He also wasn't sure how Jill would feel about that. Instead, he walked his fingers over until they brushed against hers. He felt Jill still, as her fingers sat, barely touching his.

"What about you?" she asked. "What's your life like?"

"Lots of work, like you. I've done my share of trying to prove I could do something on my own merit. That's why I want to be a success and land an acting role. Maybe one day be a leading man. To show them I can."

"Is acting really what you want to do? Say those ridiculous lines the script writer created?"

Mark laughed. She was right. Quite a few of the lines were more than ridiculous. He was quiet for a long time, just enjoying sitting next to Jill, letting his fingers touch hers. Finally, he answered, "I'm not sure. You know, I kind of envy Evan. He's got a plan. A path, it seems. I'm just..."

He wasn't sure.

"Drifting along and hoping," Jill whispered.

"Yeah." Mark looked down at her then. A sudden urge came over him to kiss her. It seemed like she did understand. And he understood her too. A part of his soul felt like it connected with hers. He could get used to that feeling.

"You know," Mark said quietly, "you aren't a bad person. I think Tara knows that, and that's why she's not mad at you."

"Do you think so?" Jill asked. She looked at him worriedly. "I don't think I've done enough. Look at them." She gestured to the small patch of woods where they could see Tara and Evan sitting close. "They're together, happy. No drama. No strife. No viewers...no assistant spot." She bit her lip. "And I'm letting my dad down."

Mark frowned. It was unfair. The amount of pressure put on her suddenly made him angry. "You're doing the best you can," he told her. "Wasn't part of the challenge to see if they would break?"

At her nod, he continued. "So far, they haven't. It's nothing you've done. Maybe they are just unbreakable. Some people are like that. So, don't feel bad. You're doing all you can."

"Maybe," Jill said doubtfully. "Maybe not." She sighed. "There's more I can do. And I will. Doesn't mean I have to like it."

She smiled at him then. "Don't tell Tara, but I'm going to play with the kitten. Outside."

Mark grinned, and watched as she coaxed the tiny ball of fur into her hands, then sat with it in her lap.

"I always wanted a kitten," Jill said, running her fingers over the silky fur.

"Any other pets?" he asked.

"None. My parents said no. Now that I'm on my own, I could have one, but I just...haven't. I'm not sure why. You?"

"Nope. Had a dog. He liked my brother better than me, so he lives with him."

Jill laughed. It was a genuinely happy one that made her eyes crinkle. He liked that. "Silly dog. I'd have chosen you," she said.

Then she seemed to realize what she said, and she blushed. Quickly, she stood. "Ah, I better put the kitten up," she said.

"Yeah, sure," Mark said.

He watched as she returned it, then couldn't help but feel a strange sensation in his stomach. It was becoming obvious to him that he liked Jill. It was also obvious that she liked him. At least a little bit.

"Hey, Mark?" Jill asked, coming back out of the cabin.

He looked at her. "What's up?"

Jill stood on her tiptoes and brushed her lips against his cheek as she whispered, "Thank you. For being here."

He grabbed her, holding her close. He didn't want to let her go. A crack of thunder sounded, followed by pelting rain. Jill gave a shriek and clung to him, her face buried in his chest. Tara and Evan ran from the woods, and Mark stepped back, letting his hands fall.

"Just so you know," he told her, as the rain hit him and a drop fell down his nose, "when we go back, when we leave here? We're friends. Hanging out together. Doing stuff. Got it?"

The smile that spread over her face warmed him as he ran back to his cabin. As Evan tore through the cabin looking for the book he'd hidden, the only thing on his mind was Jill.

When he looked through the window, Evan stood next to him. They could see the girls through their window. Tara was cooking and Jill was at the table. She looked up, caught his eyes, and blew him a kiss. Mark smiled.

Evan tensed, and Mark looked over at him, then back at the window. Tara had looked over. Understanding grew on Mark's face. Even though the kiss had been for him, Evan had thought Jill was flirting. Tara must have thought so too. Jill winked then, with that cute smirk of hers. It was obvious she'd sensed the misunderstanding too.

Though it hadn't been intentional, she'd just managed to cause a problem. Through the window, they could see Tara yelling, waving her arms about.

"Woah," Mark said, making sure the camera got his good side. "Looks like a little girl stuff going on."

"Y-yeah," Evan said, uncertainly.

Mark didn't want to do it, but he asked, trying to sound casual, "So, which of them do you like?"

"Tara, of course," Evan answered, his face one of shock. "I mean, Jill's okay. Maybe. She seems like she's trying to stir up things. I don't know why."

"It's a reality show," Mark said, clapping him on the shoulder. "You know how those are."

"Not really," Evan admitted. "I don't usually watch them."

"Oh. Same, honestly. I just was thinking about the commercials. All that drama. You know, for viewers."

"I guess," Evan said, uncertainly. "I just...I don't want things to go bad with Tara. She's the only reason I'm here. I don't want this show to cause problems. Ruin our friendship. I almost wish we'd never come. It's not been what I expected."

Evan walked away, and Mark felt a surge of guilt go through him. He couldn't imagine how bad Jill felt, flirting with Evan just because she was told to. He was about ready to tell Evan it was all a trick, a job for ratings.

But as soon as he thought that, he remembered the second round of auditions. It was a free pass. He'd be stupid to do that. So, he just held in his sigh and flopped on his bed.

Just a few more days. He could do it, right?

But one thing was for sure. He meant what he'd said. When they went back to reality, he wanted to spend more time with Jill.

A lot more time. And as more than friends.

CHAPTER 7

Jill couldn't stop shaking. It was too much. It was all too much. She reached into her pocket and wrapped her fingers around her notebook. She dug in so hard, they ached.

A half hour before, when it had gone missing, she didn't know what to think. Her mind was filled with nothing but panic. She had blown through the cabin like a tornado, looking for it. While it was unlikely anyone had seen it, she still felt scared. What if Tara really had found it, read it, and figured out she worked for the studio?

She might have just blown her cover and her chance at the assistant position.

Sure, Tara said she'd found the notebook on the ground, but Jill hadn't seen it there as she'd rushed to the barn. What if Tara was lying?

But...could Tara lie? She was so genuine. So honest. So...angry. She was still really upset at Jill, that was obvious. And why wouldn't she be? She thought Jill was trying to steal her boyfriend.

Jill groaned. That couldn't be further from the truth. Just...Tara didn't know that. Couldn't know that. Evan was alright, but he wasn't her type. He didn't make her heart thud, or bring a smile to her face by cracking a joke. He didn't look at her as though he could see her—the real her—and it didn't scare him.

Closing her eyes, Jill let herself remember Mark's fingers brushing hers. The way he'd pulled her against him. How he'd told her that when they got back, they'd be hanging out together.

It made her smile. Every bit of it. She wanted to spend more time with him. A lot of time.

She also wanted to stop feeling guilty and scared and anxious. The last few weeks had been anything but restful. At night, she laid awake worrying about Tara being upset at her, trying to think up new ways to bring tension to the show, and doing all she could to earn that interview.

"Huh?"

Tara had asked her a question. As usual, she was chattering away. Jill had gotten very good at tuning her out.

"What's the first thing you're going to do when you leave?" Tara asked.

"Shower. And then eat pizza. And cookies I didn't have to make." Jill didn't even hesitate. There was more, she was sure, but right now those were top of her list.

"Me too. And go out on a proper date with Evan. I want to see that book he found. I'm going to go see if I can borrow it."

Mark had said he'd hidden the book, and Jill hoped he had. Tara was already to the door.

"I'll go with you," Jill said.

She wasn't about to let her go alone. This could be her chance to...well, she wasn't sure. But she wasn't going to miss it. She also didn't want Tara to have a chance to talk to Evan alone. What if she told him what she'd seen in the notebook?

The rain had stopped, and there were only a few days left. She had to prove to her dad she was doing her best.

Tara's lips pressed together, but she didn't say anything as she walked toward the guys' cabin. Jill hurried behind her.

Just seconds after Tara knocked, the guys came to the door. As Tara asked about the book, Mark winked at Jill. She smiled.

Evan was shaking his head, running his fingers through his hair. Tara looked disappointed. Jill took a deep breath. If what she was about to do didn't cause some sort of drama, nothing would. Maybe Mark was right, and these two were unbreakable.

"Too bad. I wonder where it went. I guess you can't read about those courting rules now," she said, then clapped a hand over her mouth.

"Wait. I didn't say anything about that," Tara said, her eyes narrowed.

Jill quickly answered, "No, but I heard Evan talk about it." She shot him a quick glance and fluttered her lashes. Too much? Not enough? She wasn't sure. She smiled at him, trying to be seductive. "But like I said, I don't need rules to court."

Tara gasped. She looked furious. "What's wrong with you?" she asked. "Why are you doing this?"

"Doing what?" Jill asked. Her heart was pounding. Mark was shaking his head at her, making a motion to stop. Evan was looking at her in shock. She didn't know what to do.

"Everything!" Tara said, throwing her hands up. "Making everything difficult. You don't do your fair share of the chores, you go around spying on all of us and writing it down, you're flirting with Evan now, and doing it right in front of me!"

Mark stepped closer. "Let's calm down," he said.

Jill felt better with him at her side. Should she keep going? "I'm calm," Jill said with a smile. "It's Tara who seems a little—"

"Forget it," Tara interrupted. "Just forget it. It's obvious you've got something against me. Maybe you're trying to get rid of me because you think that will make you popular or you'll get my share of the prize. I don't know, but whatever it is, it won't work. I agreed to come and play by the rules, and that's what I'm going to do."

"So, does that mean without knowing the rules of the era about courting, you and Evan aren't going to date?" Jill asked, her voice sticky sweet.

Tara and Evan traded glances. He wore a concerned look on his face, while she looked angry still. Jill's mouth was dry. She hated herself right now. Hated the fear that formed on Tara's face, the tears that were threatening.

"It's okay," Evan said, interrupting her spiraling thoughts. "We are playing by the rules, all of us. Anyway, this isn't a discussion for anyone other than me and Tara to be part of."

Evan took Tara's hand and looked at her. It was obvious neither of them saw her or Mark. What would it be like to be that in love? So much so that everything else faded away? "Don't worry," he said. "We will either figure it out, or we wait a little longer until we leave. I'm okay with either, as long as I'm with you."

"But...Evan. What about you and me?" Jill tried one last time.

Tara's jaw dropped. She looked between the two of them and dropped Evan's hand. "What about you two?" she asked.

"There's nothing between us," Evan said firmly.

Mark leaned in and whispered, drowning out what Tara and Evan were saying. "Time to stop. Just let it go." He squeezed her hand.

Jill wished it made her feel better. She wished she'd stopped a moment ago. Right now, she also wished she were anywhere but here. There was a lot of wishing happening, but none of it coming true.

"Why are you doing this?" Evan was focused on her.

Jill opened her mouth, then closed it. She glanced at Mark with an uncertain look. He gave her a small head shake.

Tara narrowed her eyes. "You two are up to something," she said, pointing her finger accusingly.

"Yeah," Evan growled, crossing his arms. "What are you up to? Are you trying to force us to leave? Or force just one of us to leave? I really don't trust either of you. Jill, you are always sneaking around with that little book of yours. Mark, you do some weird stuff too. I thought I heard you talking to someone the other day. No one was there, but what I did make out, made you sound suspicious."

Neither of them answered. Jill wanted to explain, but she couldn't. Mark felt the same, she was sure, even if he wasn't in as deeply as she was. Hadn't made as many mistakes. Would Tara ever forgive her? Even when she found out the truth? Jill doubted it. She couldn't ever forgive herself.

Tara took a deep breath. "Whatever. I'm done with you. Done with all of this. This was a bad idea. I'm stupid for thinking that I'd be able to enjoy myself here, spend time with Evan and get to know him better, and have a simple, happy life for a month, leaving all the drama behind that the corporate lifestyle is filled with. Looks like I was wrong. There's drama here too, even though there didn't have to be." She spun around and stalked to the cabin, ignoring Evan calling after her.

A roaring sound filled Jill's ears. She didn't hear what Evan said to her, or Mark's answer, or anything else. She just stood, outside the cabin door, shaking, as Evan raced after Tara.

Her head felt light. Her stomach sick. Jill stumbled, and two strong arms wrapped around her, helping her to sit on a chunk of wood.

"You okay?" Mark asked.

"You know I'm not," Jill whispered. She looked up at him then, and tears fell down her face. "I wanted that job. I wanted it more than anything. But not like this. Never like this."

CHAPTER 8

Mark sat next to Jill on the ground, resting his chin on his knees. He was quiet. Honestly, he wasn't sure what to say. Was there anything he could say that wouldn't make things worse? "I know. But it is what it is."

The moment he said the words, he winced. He glanced at her, and she looked away with a scowl. Nope. That wasn't the right thing to have said. He knew it the minute it passed his lips. "That didn't come out right. I meant—"

"It's easy for you to say," she told him, sounding as though she wanted to argue.

"I know," he answered softly, reaching over and taking her hand.

He hadn't meant to reach over, but her hand, captured in his, just felt right. Jill turned to face him. Her face looked sad.

"I actually like little Miss Sunshine, if you can believe that. I went too far. This isn't who I am. If I have to move up in the company by being like this, I don't think that's what I want."

"I understand," Mark said. "I told myself it was great practice for *Hour by Hour* when I was teasing Evan earlier. It was something Lorenzo, the part I'm reading for, would do. But, like you said. That's not me. I didn't like feeling guilty, and I've done less than you. I can't even imagine how bad you feel."

"Don't remind me," Jill groaned. "The only good thing right now is that we are going home soon. We'll never have to see them again, they'll eventually find out that we were not really contestants, and maybe one day, they'll forgive me."

"Us," Mark said as he squeezed her hand. "I'm not letting you take the blame on your own. You're a good person. I know this..." he gestured with his free hand, "I don't know, troublemaking or whatever, that's not really who you are. I can tell. When this is over, I think Tara and Evan will know that too."

"Thank you," Jill said softly.

They locked eyes and Mark froze. He didn't know what to do. This wasn't ever something he'd had happen before. He always knew what to say, what to do. Right now, he had no idea. His mouth felt dry, and his chest tight. "Jill," he whispered.

She didn't answer, just moved closer.

Mark leaned in. He wasn't sure what he was about to do, kiss her or say something, when there was a shout. Evan came rushing toward them.

His words were garbled, panicked. He was pointing toward the house. "Tara," he shouted, and ran back into the cabin.

Mark and Jill scrambled to their feet. "Something's wrong," Jill said, starting to run toward the house. "Evan's acting strange."

He didn't answer. He'd seen this before as a medic. There was obviously an emergency, but until he knew what it was, time was wasting, and he couldn't spare any speculating. He also didn't want to alarm Jill.

A calm came over Mark as his medical training kicked in. He was right on Jill's heels and they burst into the cabin. A quick glimpse showed Tara in her bed, Evan hovering over her, an obvious look of panic on his face.

"What happened?" Jill asked.

"She's been stung or bitten or something. It's swelling really bad," Evan said.

Mark moved closer. He turned then, and quickly washed his hands in the bucket near the kitchen door. "Do you see a stinger?" he asked as he pulled up his sleeves.

"No," Evan said.

Mark dried his hands and hurried over. Evan was pointing. "But that's the puncture."

"I'll get cold water and a rag to put on her foot," Jill said.

Not really paying attention to the others, Mark focused on his patient. He examined Tara's rapidly swelling foot. "Single puncture, likely an insect. Perhaps a spider." He frowned, trying to recall what he'd seen here and what might have caused the bite.

His attention moved to Tara, and she started shivering. "I'm so cold," she whispered. Her eyes weren't focusing on him, which was worrying.

Mark touched her head. "You're clammy."

Evan was right at his shoulder. He'd been there crowding him. Mark needed space to think. How could he get rid of him for a moment? It was obvious Evan was worried, he didn't fault him for that, but he needed space.

He knew Evan didn't know he was a medic, and here for this very reason. Should he tell him? It was difficult to tell how serious the situation was.

"Evan, go get our blankets." Mark pointed at the door.

Evan rushed out of the cabin, and Mark took a breath. "Finally. Elbow room." He looked at Jill. "Got those cloths?"

"I do." Jill laid the cool cloth on Tara's ankle. "Will this help?"

"I really don't know," Mark said. He shook his head. "Honestly, I don't think so. I think I'll need to get the emergency kit and call for help."

"How will we do that? The cameras?" Jill asked. She looked to where one was. "We need help! Get a doctor."

"There's also an emergency radio," Mark said. Evan walked in then, preventing him from saying anything else. It was going to be time soon to make a choice—let Evan know who they were and get help, or manage it on his own. How long could he do that?

"This isn't good," Jill whispered, and looked at Mark.

He agreed. Tara was sweaty, her face was pale, and she let out a moan. As if the kitten knew something was wrong, she jumped up on Tara's chest and started crying.

Mark checked Tara's pulse. "It's too fast," he said. "I wish I knew what bit her. It's so swollen, I can't tell. My instinct is a spider. We are in the woods and there aren't many flying things with stingers around here."

"She's very flushed," Jill said. "Her breathing doesn't seem right. I think she's having an allergic reaction."

He agreed. He had to get the supplies from the barn and radio for help. It didn't matter now if Evan saw. The concern was helping Tara. Every moment he delayed could be critical. "Be right back," Mark said.

"Where are you going?" Evan asked.

Mark hesitated. He and Jill traded glances. She gave a small nod, and so he answered. If the boss's daughter gave the okay, it was good enough for him. He paused near the door. "Emergency first aid kit."

"We have an emergency first aid kit? Is it a modern one? Or some weird 1800s stuff?" Evan jumped up to follow him, but Jill stopped him.

"Let him go alone," she said.

Even looked like he was going to argue, but Mark didn't hang around to listen. He hurried to the barn. In a back corner were four crates. Two were empty, there only as props. In the third was the radio and emergency batteries. He snapped one in and pressed the button.

"This is 1800s Experiment. Mark speaking. We have a medical emergency."

He pulled his thumb from the radio button and listened to the static. He didn't have to wait long. A voice replied, "Hey, Mark. It's Joe. Don't worry, we're sending out a doctor now. You should have enough supplies to treat Tara until he gets there."

"I'm getting it now," Mark told him, relief filling him that Joe had answered quickly.

"Hey, by the way," Joe crackled. "I liked those lines you were feeding the cow recently."

"Shut up," Mark growled. "This isn't the time."

"Alright. But, for what it's worth, you'd make a great Lorenzo."

Mark chuckled. He finally pried the nails off the final crate and pulled out a large medical backpack. There were a few other things inside too. Better to take it all.

"I'm going back in," Mark said. "I'm shutting off the radio."

He clicked it off and hurried to the house. A thought flitted through his mind. At times, he'd forgotten all about the camera. That meant earlier, when he'd almost kissed Jill...

But there was no time to think about that. Tara needed help.

Mark carried in the large crate. He set it on the floor and opened the lid. Evan started hovering again.

He glanced at Tara, then began to organize what he needed and what he needed to do in his mind. How well stocked was the kit? "I've got things to bandage," he said, riffling through, "and a small knife if we need to drain the wound. I'm not sure either of those are the best thing right now. Here's some ointment." He made a small pile on the floor, and pushed the things he didn't want to one side of the box.

"What about epinephrine?" Jill asked. "Antihistamines? Those should be there as well. Look for a small pouch."

"Epinephrine?" Evan asked, his head darting between the two of them. "What are you talking about? And who are you really?"

Ignoring him, Mark pulled out a small red case and dropped a blood pressure cuff and stethoscope next to it. "Yes, there are four EpiPens right here. I've also got prednisone and antihistamines. I'll administer the steroid and antihistamine first. I don't think she's in anaphylaxis, but I'll be ready."

As he moved toward Tara, Evan grabbed his arm. "Hold it. You aren't doing anything until you talk to me first," he said.

Jill moved closer, ready to help him if he needed it. Mark wondered if he'd have to lock Evan outside or tie him to a chair. Evan was getting upset. If he couldn't calm him, he'd have to do that in order to get Tara the help she needed.

Calmly, Mark answered, "Evan, I'm a medic. I do this every day. Tara seems to have started with a mild allergic reaction, but it's growing past that. If it progresses, then we will need to treat her in order to make sure she recovers. The best way to do that is to treat her now and see if she responds, and if not, treat her aggressively with what we have until we can get help."

To his relief, Evan stepped aside. Mark hurried back over to the bed. He measured out pills into his hand from the various small containers. "Tara? Can you hear me? I need you to swallow this medicine."

Tara let out a soft moan, but she cracked open her lips slightly.

Glancing around for Jill, Mark spotted her. "Give me some water."

Jill had it in his hand in a moment. He put the pills in Tara's mouth and dribbled water in. He watched as she swallowed, then checked her mouth with his small flashlight.

Another small sound, almost a whimper, came from Tara.

"It's okay," Jill said, her voice soothing. She reached over and took Tara's hand. "We've got this. Mark knows just what to do, and help is on the way. You're going to be just fine."

Evan started to pace. It was distracting. Jill seemed to realize this. With a glance at Mark, Jill stood and followed Evan, then put her hand on his arm to stop him. "What if she's not?" he whispered, but not very quietly. "We're here without any help. Without any way to contact someone."

"That's not true," Jill said. Her voice was reassuring, her head calm. Mark appreciated it. You never knew how someone would respond in an emergency. "Remember the cameras? Once Tara started having problems, the person watching the screens would have called for help."

"I don't know what's worse," Evan groaned. He put both hands on his head. "Her being sick right now, or how she's going to act when she wakes up in a hospital, this close to winning."

Mark glanced at Jill. She looked startled, obviously feeling the same way he did. He'd been so focused, and rightly so, on Tara's medical need, he'd forgotten just how much she was enjoying being here and that for her and Evan, this wasn't just a game. It was a life changing

opportunity, just a little differently than it was for him or Ji
ll.

Evan had moved back to Tara and was talking quietly to
her. Jill put her hand on Mark's arm.

"We've got to do something to help them," she
whispered. "We've got to make sure they can make it. They
are so close. Do you think she can be treated here?"

Mark glanced at Tara. He honestly didn't know. "I'd like
a second opinion," he said quietly. "My job is to get the
help they need. Not to make the medical decisions. I don't
have the training that a doctor would have."

"One's on the way, right?" she whispered.

"There you go again," Evan interrupted, irritation thick
in his voice. "Keeping secrets." He glared at them from
Tara's bedside.

"Not in a bad way," Jill said, holding out her hands in a
pleading gesture. "I promise."

Her soft tone and stance didn't seem to matter. Evan
sprang up, his voice filled with anger, though he tried to
keep quiet for Tara. "I'm sick of this," Evan said. "Why
can't you just tell us what's going on?"

Mark stepped forward, putting himself alongside of Jill.
"I promise we will as soon as Tara wakes up." He glanced at
Jill. Her tiny nod showed they were in agreement. "You're
right. You deserve to know the truth."

CHAPTER 9

Jill calmly stirred the pot on the cookstove. However, she felt anything but calm. The little bubbles simmering in the pot were a mirror to her emotions. There was a lot bubbling up in her, too.

Fear.

Regret.

Sadness.

Mark walked in and stood next to her. "A doctor will be here any moment," he said. "He's not far."

"Good," she said.

"None of this is good," Evan said.

She glanced over, and went closer. "She's looking a little better," Jill offered.

"I'm not talking to you," Evan told her. "You've done enough. Same with you," he said, looking over at Mark.

Mark shrugged. "We've just been doing our jobs," he said.

"You'd better explain what that means," Evan said tensely. "Tara could be dying right now. She's my focus. Later, it'll be you two. And there better be a lot of explanations involved."

"I'll go wait outside for the doctor," Jill said, then left without waiting for a reply.

She settled at the table outside and rested her chin in a hand. She couldn't wait to get home. After a long, hot shower and takeout, she'd stay in bed for a week. A month. Then she wouldn't have to see anyone.

She already knew when the show aired, she wouldn't be watching. The thought of seeing herself on the screen, and reliving all of the things she'd done to push Tara and Evan wasn't very appealing. When it aired, could she even show her face in public? Jill wasn't sure.

The door opened, then closed, and she looked over to see Mark. He plopped down next to her. "Should you be out here?" she asked.

"She's sleeping right now, and Evan's right there. I wanted to check on you a moment. Luckily, the doctor will be here soon." Mark glanced at her. "So, how are you?"

"I'm fine. I'm not the one who got bitten." Jill didn't meet his gaze.

"No, you aren't. But I can tell you feel bad."

"Of course I do," she told him. "I mean...maybe if she hadn't gotten mad at me, she wouldn't have stalked off and gotten bitten. The whatever it was might have scurried away."

"Yeah," he agreed, "or maybe it would have gotten someone else. You don't know. You can't blame yourself for her."

"I don't. I blame myself for doing my job, and feeling guilty about it." Tara sighed. "I hope the doctor hurries."

"Me too." Mark moved closer to her.

They were quiet for a few minutes, then Mark said, "I don't know what it's like to have all that family pressure, but I do know what it's like to put pressure on yourself. Do you know why I want to act?"

She looked at him and shook her head. "No. A lot of people want to, so I guess I never thought much about it."

"It's simple. I want to do something I thought I might enjoy." At her surprised look, he continued, "My whole life, I've done stuff for others. I've looked after others. I've been the legal caregiver since I was eighteen for my two younger siblings. Before that, I was pretty much their caregiver anyway, when I was twelve and the three of us got taken in by a foster home.

"We bounced around place to place, and sometimes we weren't even all together. I knew that wasn't what I wanted for us, so as soon as I could, I adopted them."

When Mark sighed, Jill reached over and slid her hand into his, and rested her head on his shoulder. "That must have been so hard," she told him.

"It really was. I had no idea how to be a parent. I didn't really have a great role model. But do you know what I did have?" he told her with a laugh.

"What?" she asked.

"*Hour by Hour*. I got hooked on it as a teen. One of my favorite storylines was the guy who pulled himself up out of nothing, by acting. My other favorite storyline was the one about the guy who grew up an orphan and became a doctor. So, as crazy as it sounds, I went to college and studied acting and also had paramedic training. That's why the job at the studio was perfect. A chance to act, also a job as a paramedic."

Jill couldn't stop the smile that formed. "I had no idea that a show could influence someone so much," she said. "Wow. That's amazing, really."

"Sounds silly," he laughed. "But it worked for me. That example was what I needed as a kid, and I took it. And now, I'm here."

Mark looked at her, his face suddenly very serious. "I'm going to do all I can to help Tara, and I need you to do the same and not worry about what others think about you. Not them, not your dad, not the people back at the studio, or even strangers. Be you. Unapologetically. You're an incredible person, and I'm so glad I said yes to coming here. I—"

The unwelcome sound of a vehicle stopped Mark, and they both stood as an SUV pulled up.

A doctor jumped out, and Mark jogged over to help carry the two large bags he was pulling from the back.

Jill followed behind, listening as the doctor looked over Tara. Evan seemed more relaxed now, especially as he'd heard that Mark had done the right things and had the situation under control.

She glanced at Tara, then turned away, stirring the large pot again. She couldn't help with the medical side of things, but she could make meals and keep everyone fed so it was one less worry.

Her eyes fell on some apples, and she cleaned them, then sliced them, dropped them in a large pot and added a little water, butter, and cinnamon. It sounded like it would work well, anyway. Hopefully it would. Before she put the lid on, she added a small sprinkle of brown sugar.

The doctor came over. "I have a letter for you," he told her.

Jill wiped her hands on her apron and took it. She recognized the handwriting. But, why would her dad be writing her now? She'd be seeing him soon. She opened the envelope and skimmed the letter.

"Mark," she said. When he came over, she handed him the letter, and watched as his eyebrows rose.

"Well then. That's a surprise," he said, and handed her back the letter.

Jill nodded, trying to ignore the glare Evan was giving her. Hopefully, he wouldn't be as upset once Tara woke up and she explained everything to them.

The evening dragged on. Everyone ate, and her apple concoction didn't turn out too badly. Jill yawned, getting tired. The sun was starting to set. Mark came in from checking on the animals.

The doctor was examining Tara again. A few minutes later, there was a flurry of activity, and she looked up from the bread dough she was making. Tara was awake.

Jill moved closer, a little worried what the other girl's response would be when she saw her. Mark sensed her hesitation and moved closer.

The doctor excused himself to go report back to the studio. Jill felt a little envious. She knew he could feel the tension in the room, and not over Tara's bite.

When he was gone, Tara frowned at her. "I have questions I want answers to," she said.

"Same," Evan said.

"We'll tell you everything now," Mark promised, dragging a chair near the bed.

"We? So you are in on all the weird stuff," Evan said, sitting back slightly.

"Sort of," Mark said. He hesitated.

Jill shrugged. "No sort of," she admitted, bringing her own chair over. "We were in on it. But it's for a good reason," she said, holding up a hand to stall Evan's protest he had forming. His eyes were narrowed, and were practically shooting darts at her.

"We're listening," Tara said. She crossed her arms. The kitten walked up her chest, and Tara uncrossed her arms to stroke its fur.

"Okay," Mark said. "Well, we work for the station."

"What?" Tara gasped. Snowball startled and nearly fell off the bed. Jill caught him, gave a little nuzzle, and handed him back to Tara.

"Yeah. The head producer is my dad. It's a long story, I'll tell you later, but basically, the only way I could actually work for the station and not get accused of nepotism was to take an intern spot, ace it, and then start moving up the ranks. Hello intern spot," she said, waving her arm around. "I hate the outdoors, so whoever thought I'd be perfect for this, well, I hope for their sake I never find out."

"What's your story?" Evan asked, glancing at Mark. His look was one of confusion now. She didn't blame him. Not only was it a lot to take in, right now it probably sounded strange.

"I took the job because what I really want is to audition for a role on the soap opera *Hour by Hour*. The chores have really buffed up my body," Mark added, flexing, "so

I'm really hoping when we get back to get through the auditions and land that role."

"A soap opera?" Tara stared at him, and her jaw dropped.

"Not just any soap," Mark argued. "It's *Hour by Hour*. That show's been running for decades, and has churned out more actors and actresses who've gone on to be successful on shows and movies than any other show."

"If you say so," Evan said, his eyebrows raised.

"I'll also pay off my student loans for college," Mark said. He shrugged. "If I get the part, anyway. I've got a backup plan if I don't. Something medicine related."

"So, that's it? Jill flirted with Evan and didn't do chores, and Mark did it all to what...increase the drama and gain muscle?" Tara looked skeptical.

Jill crinkled her nose and grimaced. "Okay, when you say it that way, we kinda sound awful. I promise, we aren't. Anyway! There's something we've been just dying to tell you. Remember how the producer said there was an extra prize that could be won?" Jill asked.

She jumped up and pulled the letter from her pocket. She didn't want to mess this up. After everything that had happened, she was thrilled to be able to offer this to Evan and Tara.

Mark stood up too, and grinned. "We just got told about it. It's a big one. Big, big prize. And we think you two will be perfect for it."

"Wanna spit it out already?" Tara asked, scowling.

With a grin splitting her face, Jill burst out, "What would you say if I told you that you two had the opportunity to live here for an entire year?"

Now it was Evan and Tara who traded looks. There was a flash of surprise, something that looked worried, and then one of confusion.

"You are leaving something out," Tara finally said and she glanced back at Jill. "I sense it. Spit it out. All of it. Don't leave anything out."

Mark jumped in, and gestured. "This place is about twenty-five acres. There's the barn, this cabin, and the smaller one. All the animals, the supplies, a wagon and horses. Everything here, lock, stock, and barrel is all yours for the keeping, free and clear, along with the hundred thousand dollars each, plus another hundred and fifty thousand each, if you can live here for a year like you are in the 1800s."

"A year?" Tara gasped.

Jill didn't miss Evan's look. He appeared terrified.

She laughed. "Yeah. The catch is just you two, though. Mark and I aren't doing it. No way," Jill said. She made a giant X with her hands.

"It would all be ours? Forever?" Tara asked. Her voice was near a whisper.

Jill nodded. Tara's face had softened. Jill hesitated, then reached out her hand to squeeze her arm. "That's right.

All yours. Your dream, Tara. To live like this. And after that year, you can do anything you want. You can put in plumbing. You can get electricity. You can do anything you want."

"You'd have an entire year to figure out what you want to have, and what you are happy with," Mark added. He clapped Evan on the shoulder.

"What about the cameras?" Tara asked.

"Only in the barn, the kitchen, public places like that," Jill assured her. "And that way, if there's another medical emergency, you can get help."

"Wait, wait, wait," Evan said. "What about your job? Your family? The hard work here?" He still seemed in shock as he asked Tara.

"What about the fact I could live the life I've always wanted to and have an incredible financial future for my family one day?" Tara asked. "Do you know how long and how hard I'd have to work to save up to buy a place like this, and the two hundred and fifty grand on top? How many mind-numbing hours I'd need to spend? Rent isn't cheap, neither is what I pay to commute to work each week."

"I hadn't thought of that," Evan said. "That's a lot of hours looking at data sheets." He grimaced. "A lot of hours."

"And meetings," Tara told him. "Endless meetings and clients and pressure to meet deadlines."

"I see why this is appealing," Evan admitted. "I hate those meetings. And those data sheets. Are you thinking it's a yes, then?"

"I would love to do it," Tara said. "I know you might not want to. And I know it isn't fair of me to ask you to stay if you don't want to."

"I want to think about it," Evan said slowly. "There's a lot then I'd have to do. That evil cow won't milk herself," he added. The others laughed and he shrugged. Apologetically, he said, "I'm not sure really if just the two of us could manage this place. And what if you needed me and I'm all the way in the other house asleep? I need to think this through. Do what's best. We were going to plan a future together, remember? A little hard to do that if we're on camera for a year."

Jill was starting to tear up. She didn't didn't miss the flash of sadness in Tara's eyes. She couldn't help but sniffle. It was like a live episode of a soap opera playing before her.

"Of course," Tara said, quickly. "I understand completely."

Jill didn't want to interrupt, but she also couldn't stop staring. She knew she ought to step back, give them privacy. But when she darted her eyes away for a moment, she saw Mark also staring, hardly unable to look away.

"The problem," Evan said slowly, "is that if I stay, it can't be like it is right now."

"What do you mean?" Jill asked. She frowned. Had he not understood what she said? She pulled out the letter to show him. "You'd need to live here like it's the 1800s."

"Yes," Evan said. "That part I get."

Jill tuned them out a moment as the doctor moved outside of the window and drew her attention. When she looked back, Mark was talking.

Mark nodded. "Yes. Unless you—"

"It's good, man. I've got this part," Evan said, winking at him.

Tara blinked at him, looking confused. "What?"

Jill felt confused too. What had she missed? She'd only looked away a moment. Then, it hit her and her eyes widened.

"Unless I did this," Evan asked.

Jill gasped and then jumped up and down as he dropped onto a knee and took Tara's hand.

"Will you marry me? And we will spend the next year living like crazy people in the middle of nowhere with no running water or electricity and loving every minute of it?"

"Yes!" Tara squealed and wrapped her arms around him tightly. "Oh, my gosh! I always wanted an 1800s wedding gown!"

Jill wiped at her eyes. They'd gotten so misty. She and Mark stepped away to the kitchen area to give the two a moment of privacy. The doctor walked in then, and Mark went outside with him. Jill followed them and the doctor explained he'd stay for a few days to keep an eye on Tara.

"I'm going to check her again," he said, returning to the cabin.

Jill and Mark stayed outside. Jill smiled at Mark, then looked up at the sky, where small stars were starting to show.

"We made it," Mark said. "In a few hours, we're done. They've got the opportunity of a lifetime, we do too. Tara and Evan got what they wanted in regards to moving forward with their relationship, you rocked the boat and they didn't fall out." He grinned at her. "That's good for ratings. You've got your job interview, I've got my audition, and everyone's alive and hopefully still somewhat friends. I'd say that about summed up the last four weeks."

"You missed a few things," Jill said wryly, "but overall, I approve of your assessment. It seems Tara isn't upset at me anymore either. So, that's honestly a huge relief."

Mark put her arm around her, and Jill leaned against him. She could get used to this. Very, very used to it. When they went back home, would he ever do this? Would they ever see each other?

She wasn't sure how long they stood there, silent but close. Eventually, the sound of vehicles pulled her away. A lump formed in Jill's throat. This was it. Their ride home.

She hadn't wanted to be there at all, now she wasn't sure she was ready to leave.

Chapter 10

"Well, I'm proud of you both," the producer, Jill's father, said as he sat across from them at his desk. "Well done. I know it wasn't easy, but you pulled it off."

Mark nodded, and let his mind wander. In the last twenty-four hours they'd gone from living in the 1800s to a few hundred years later. It had felt strange to ride in a car again, but he'd quickly adapted. A hot shower, double pepperoni pizza, and a soft bed had quickly welcomed him back.

Judging by Jill's new appearance, she felt the same. It was a little strange seeing her not in one of those flowery dresses the girls had to wear. She was in jeans, a black tee, and had her hair loose, instead of pulled back into the low 1800s bun he'd gotten used to.

"I hope you don't mind meeting at the same time," the producer continued. "I'm afraid I've got a lot of meetings today."

"No problem, Mr. Masterson," Mark said.

"Yep. No problem," Jill said. She took a sip from the cup she'd carried in. One of her feet were taping nervously. Mark looked down and saw he'd been tapping one of his fingers. Looked like they were both feeling a little anxious.

"The footage has turned out great. Everyone looks good on camera, there's enough interesting stuff for the history buffs, but a little drama for those who'd expect that from a reality show," the producer continued.

He fixed his eyes on Jill. "They didn't seem to rattle too easily, did they?"

"I did my best," Jill said. "Their relationship seemed pretty firm, though. Honestly, a few times I was a little worried about their reactions. I'm glad Mark was there." She gave a small laugh, but Mark could hear the worry in it

.

Her father seemed to hear it as well. He nodded. "You did well," he told her.

"Dad," Jill said, "I mean, Mr. Masterson, I don't ever want to do anything like that again. Not the great outdoors, but more importantly, not being mean or spreading lies on a show. That's just not me."

"I know, hon. I had to have someone there I could trust, someone who would take it far enough, but not too far.

But no, no more of that." The producer leaned back in his chair. "So, about your prizes."

Mark held his breath. He could hear Jill as she sucked in hers. The producer nodded at them. "Jill, the interview is yours. It's day after tomorrow at ten. It's a formality, really, but take it seriously. Show them what you are made of."

He looked at Mark next. "I saw a few of the shots with you practicing your lines," he said. A smile twitched at the corners. "The cow was an unusual choice of partners, but you did well. Your audition is tomorrow at eight."

"Second round?" Mark asked.

"Second round." Mr. Masterson looked over at his phone, which had lit up. "I've got to take this. Good luck, you two."

Mark stood and waited for Jill to leave first. When they got into the hallway, she sagged against the wall. "Oh my gosh. I hate going in there."

"He's your dad," Mark said.

"Yeah. And each time I go in there, it's like I'm a kid in the principal's office."

He laughed. "Good luck with your interview."

"You too." Jill smiled at him. "If you get the role, maybe I'll get to see more of you on set."

"That would be—" his radio crackled.

"Medics to set four. The animatronic shark just bit someone."

Jill raised her eyebrows. "That sounds...worrying."

Mark laughed. "Yep." He hefted his medical backpack. "I'll see you later."

"See you."

When he turned at the hallway, Jill was still watching him, and gave a little wave. He grinned, waved, then broke into a full run to get to set four.

A few hours later, he headed home, glad the day was over. The rest of the night was spent practicing his lines, and he was too nervous to sleep. Worried he'd miss the audition, he made sure to get to the studio at seven.

Before a group of bleary-eyed casting staff, nearly twenty people read lines. Mark jumped up the moment his name was called. He stepped in front of one of the *Hour by Hour* stars, Lena. Lena played a rich socialite, and stayed in character both on and off the set. A lot of people didn't like her because of that.

"Now, don't be nervous," Lena purred. "Just let me see what you can do, handsome."

"Right." Mark cleared his throat, and waited for the head casting producer's nod. When she did, he reached for Lena's hand. "I...I couldn't help it," he said quietly. "When I saw your beauty, I took leave of my senses. I had no idea that I would get temporary amnesia after wrestling the bear that escaped from the forest to save that group of girl scouts. Or that you had a twin sister, with a birthmark in the exact same place. As she was nursing me back to health, spoon feeding me broth, I..." Mark tossed his head, hoping he had enough smolder, "was thinking of you the whole time. You are the only one for me, Lena. I've known it from the moment we met."

The words startled him. So much so, that when Lena continued with her lines, he couldn't hear her. When she turned back to him, fluttering her eyelashes, he regained his focus, and said, "As long as the days are long, and the sodas from McFizzy are carbonated, you...will...always..." he brought the smolder again, "be the one I love."

There was a smattering of applause, and Lena smiled at him. "My, my, that was very good."

"We'll let you know," the producer said. "Next."

Mark turned to leave. A familiar person was waiting outside the set. "Hey," he said in surprise.

"Hey," Jill repeated, then she put her hand to her forehead, and in a breathy voice said, "As long as the days are long, and the sodas from McFizzy are carbonated..."

"Hey!" Mark interrupted. "I brought the smolder, thank you. And my voice wasn't whispery. It was pleading. Commanding. I hope, anyway."

She laughed. "It was great. I was just teasing. I can't stand Lena."

"You and almost everyone else," Mark said. "That's why the ratings are so high."

"She does her job well," Jill agreed. She looked away for a moment. "Honestly, your lines were too good. It sounded real."

Mark felt his heart start to speed up. "You know," he said, grabbing her hand and starting to walk down the hallway, "it was actually hard because the whole time I was looking at Lena, there was only one person I wanted to say those lines to."

"About the McFizzy?" Jill smirked at him.

Mark stopped, and faced her. "Yes. No. You are the only one for me, Jill. I've known it from the moment we met. But," he added, looking down a moment, and tossing his head up for the smolder, "As long as the days are long, and the sodas from McFizzy are carbonated, you will always be the one I want to spend time with."

She didn't answer. There was no smirk, no smile, just a shocked expression. It made him feel nervous.

"Really?" she finally asked.

"Really," Mark said. "Will you go out with me this weekend?"

"Where to?" Jill asked, wrapping her arm through his as they started walking toward the break room.

"On a date. To the SPCA. They just got a litter of kittens. I want to get you one."

"Really?" Jill squealed. She threw her arms around his neck and squeezed him so tightly his vision dimmed and he gasped for air. "Really," he choked out.

"I'd love to," Jill said. She released him, then smiled. "As long as the days are long and the sodas from McFizzy are carbonated, you will also always be the one I want to spend time with. You and my new kitten."

EPILOGUE

"Hey! You stole my pepperoni," Mark complained.

"Give it back, you naughty kitten," Jill said, shaking her finger at the gray, grumpy faced kitty. "That wasn't nice, Thumper."

"Ugh, he can keep it," Mark grumbled. "It's half gone, now." He switched through the TV channels.

Jill took up her slice again. "Do you know, in just two days, Tara and Evan will have made it a year."

"I can hardly believe how fast time has gone," Mark said. He picked up his soda. "Think they'll stay?"

"Oh yeah," Jill said. "Without a doubt."

They'd gotten to watch some of the footage, and it looked like Tara and Evan were doing just fine.

Things had been going pretty well for her and Mark too. They'd been dating almost a year, and who knows, something more official might be on the horizon for them too, one day.

In the meantime, she'd been enjoying her job in casting, and he was cast as Lorenzo, on *Hour by Hour*, just like he'd hoped for.

"Hey," Mark said, landing on a medical show. "I want to ask you something. Well, two somethings."

"This sounds serious," Jill said, looking at him in concern.

"It is. Sort of." Mark started to pull crumbs from his pizza crust. "It's *Hour by Hour*. You know, I know it's what I wanted. What I thought I wanted. But, would you still like me even if I wasn't on the screen in front of thousands of viewers?"

"Of course I would," Jill said. "Why?"

"I realized acting isn't what I really want. I want to go to medical school to be a doctor or a nurse. I like helping give others the care they need."

Jill fought to keep the giggles from her voice. "So, playing Lorenzo, and performing a successful appendectomy with only a ballpoint pen and a pair of nail clippers isn't the kind of medical thing you want to keep doing? You want the real thing?"

"Ugh. Where do they come up with this stuff?" Mark grunted. "No, Lorenzo is about to be eaten by that animatronic shark. So, I was given a choice. Sign a new contract and be his evil twin brother who is a basketball player turned cowboy, or find something new."

"Whatever you want, I'll support you on," Jill said.

"I was hoping you'd say that," Mark grinned. "And there's one more thing I'm hoping you'd say yes to."

"What's that?" Jill asked. She picked up her drink. Mark grinned, and she narrowed her eyes. "What are you up to?"

Dropping his head, he suddenly looked up with the smolder. "As long as the days are long and the sodas from McFizzy are carbonated, you will always be the one I want to spend time with. Jill, will you marry me?"

"Yes, yes I will," Jill said, and she wrapped her arms around his neck. "You know, this is great timing."

"How so?" Mark asked suspiciously.

"Ever wanted an 1800s wedding? Dad's casting for a new show to build a town and—"

"Never again!" Mark groaned, smacking his hands over his ear. "Never, ever again!"

WANT THE OTHER SIDE OF THE STORY? FIND TARA AND EVAN ON AMAZON!

Thrilled to be chosen as a reality show contestant, Tara is even more excited her best friend Evan will be with her. She's looking forward to getting away and relaxing. Though life seems perfect on the outside, it's anything but. So a huge cash prize for pretending she's in her favorite time period and time to figure life out? Sounds great to her!

Evan would do anything for Tara. Including living in the middle of nowhere as though it were the 1800s. It feels like the perfect time to take their relationship to the next level, and he can't imagine a better place than Tara's dream setting. Until he realizes just how many rules there were back then with relationships. Just one more thing to add to the list of complications as of late.

With a life-changing amount of money if they just make it those four weeks, Tara and Evan are determined to survive the worst the 1800s can throw at them—no plumbing, angry barn animals, dangers of rural living, rules around romance—and come out winners.

But the other couple with them, Jill and Mark, seem like they are up to something. Could it spell disaster for Tara and Evan's relationship? It might just be this 1800s experiment is far more than either bargained for.

https://www.amazon.com/gp/product/B0CVV8367B

Chapter 1

Tara James scanned the seemingly endless emails in her inbox. One of these days she'd do a massive deep clean out. She was sure she didn't even remember signing up for half of the junky newsletters in there. Why didn't she ever get anything good?

In between the usual mass of offers to buy a car warranty or claim her inheritance as the only relative from a prince in some non-existent country, something caught her eye. She blinked a few times, but it still read the same—*Finalist for 1800s Survival Challenge!*

"What? No way," she muttered, and clicked on the email. It seemed to take forever to load. "Come on, hurry up," she said to her ancient computer.

One day while at the mall, there had been someone passing out audition applications for a new reality TV series. Lured by the premise, she and Evan, her almost boyfriend, had signed up for it. It wasn't just the form they'd filled out, but each had given a quick on camera interview.

The show was seeing if modern day people could survive a month living like they were in the 1800s. No internet, no phones, no electricity, no indoor plumbing. Honestly, it didn't sound too bad to Tara. Well, except for the indoor plumbing. She enjoyed that perk of this time period. The rest, she was sure she could handle easily. Books, movies, it didn't matter, she loved it. The slower time, the people who seemed to enjoy each moment, felt content at the end of the day, built lasting relationships with those around them...it would be kind of fun to live l ike that.

Holding her breath, she read the email carefully, then read it again. It looked pretty legit. Was it? There was only one way to know. Grabbing her phone, she sent a text to Evan. Had he gotten one too?

Hey, just got an email. Remember that show we signed up for? They picked me!

She didn't have to wait long before her phone pinged.

Same! Think we might win? Will we get to work together?

Don't know. Would be fun!

It would also be a little tricky to take that much time off of work, so Tara figured she'd best go check in with her boss now. Evan was likely doing the same. She scooped up the files that she needed to drop off anyway, and headed over to Lindsay's office.

Lindsay Madison, her best friend since middle school, was also her boss. Well, second in command of the place but still her boss. After college, where she had studied fashion design, Tara had applied for an intern position with Lindsay's mom's company: Madison Apparel. They designed medical uniforms. Not exactly the high fashion she'd hoped for as a teen, but she really enjoyed it, and in two short years had worked herself up in the company.

Now, at twenty-four, she was in charge of selecting the fabric from suppliers and helping redesign their entire line this year. It was a big deal. And one that she relished being part of.

But sometimes...no, if she was being honest with herself, a lot of times, it felt like something was missing. She was getting tired of trying to figure out what it was. Maybe the chance to live simply, to think and focus on her life, would help her narrow in on it.

Every day had felt like the same since the newness of the job wore off. There were endless emails, a frantic pace to keep up with, clients to make happy, suppliers to keep on schedule, designs to sketch out to encourage people to buy their new apparel right now, and from them.

Tara passed a cluster of interns arguing over a design they'd been asked to create. They looked upset and frustrated and she completely understood. Tara shook her head. *Glad that's not me anymore.*

When she first started working there, she wondered, how much pizazz can you really put into scrubs, or how different could you make them to convince people that they had to have the newest designs in your catalog?

It was surprisingly stressful, and even though it was her job, a small part of her also didn't like the idea of telling people to buy new things all the time, acting like the new version was so much better when it really wasn't.

At a meeting this morning, she wanted to ask why it was so important to encourage slate-gray uniforms to replace the steel-gray ones that a major company had bought last year, but she held her tongue. After all, this was what paid the bills. There was just an uncomfortable feeling inside of her though, and she didn't like it.

Was it really that she didn't like to sell to people? That she simply wanted to design? Or was it something else? That feeling of not being content with her life had been happening more and more. She couldn't help but wonder if there was something better, more fulfilling, waiting for her.

Tara stopped outside of Lindsay's open door and tapped. Her friend looked up, the phone in her hand, and waved her in. "I don't care what you need to do to make it happen," she said to whoever it was on the phone. "Those catalogs need to be shipped by the end of the week and our website updated. Call me tomorrow with a status report."

Lindsay hung up, and smiled at her friend. "Thanks," she said, as Tara set down the files.

"No problem," Tara answered, then took a moment to enjoy the view. Lindsay had a small office, but it was a corner one. Though only a few stories high, from her windows the bustling city beckoned, with perfectly manicured lawns and trees along with flowers in their beds.

"It's beautiful, isn't it?" Lindsay said, nodding at the park. "They just planted the pink flowers over there, whatever they are."

"It is. But it's almost too perfect." Tara crinkled her nose as she eyed the landscape critically. It really was. Flowers were planted in perfect rows, the trees were all trimmed to the same shape, and everything looked as though it had been done in some precise way designed by someone with an architectural degree. Even the park benches each sat in the same direction.

Lindsay laughed. "That is so you," she exclaimed.

"Can I help it if I prefer natural landscapes?" Tara shrugged. "There's just something amazing about nature's own beauty. It doesn't have anyone telling it what to do or how to be, restraining a tree and making it only grow in one direction, even if it was meant to be in another. Have you ever seen a field full of wild flowers? Or tall grasses waving in the breeze? It's breathtaking."

Lindsay shook her head. "Now you just sound weird. What have you been reading? Another historical fiction? Can you imagine what those people had to go through way back when in the olden days? Books and movies make that stuff sound better than it is, you know. Those people all had to pee in the woods. Or in a pot they emptied."

"Yeah, I know," Tara said. "But there was good stuff too."

"Like what?" Lindsay asked. She shook her head. "No way, we've made progress. You couldn't pay me to live back then, even if some of those actors in Regency movies are swoony."

Tara knew that her friend didn't fully share the same tastes as she did in books or movies. In her leisure time, she enjoyed watching TV shows like *Little House on the Prairie* and *Dr. Quinn Medicine Woman*. She also enjoyed reading novels that were set in that time period. In the summer, she had a garden and was teaching herself to crochet. So what? Everyone had something they enjoyed. That didn't make her weird, even if others might think those were old-fashioned hobbies.

"It was a lot of work back then," she agreed finally, "but there always seemed to be such a happiness and satisfaction at the end of the day."

"Don't you feel that now?" Lindsay asked, raising her eyebrows. "You work just as hard as anyone here. Maybe even harder at times. Did you not just sell thirty thousand uniforms to one of the largest hospital systems in the East?"

"I guess," Tara said reluctantly. "But something just feels different as of late. It's like I'm wondering if I'm doing the right thing with my life. I mean, today I had to spend nearly an hour convincing someone that the uniforms they bought a few months ago weren't nearly as good as the almost identical ones we are offering this year. It's...I don't want to say soul sucking, but it's...I don't know. I don't feel as happy as I used to."

Tara stopped the sigh she was feeling. Lindsay didn't understand. This was her life. She'd grown up with this, and the puzzled look on her face said she didn't understand why Tara didn't enjoy what she was doing. Tara decided to press ahead. "Anyway, that's kind of what I wanted to talk with you about."

"Oh?" Lindsay asked. "What's up?" She sat behind her desk, reached for her coffee mug and took a sip.

Tara took the chair across from her, and squeezed her hands together, suddenly nervous. "I need a favor. It's about Evan, too."

"Don't tell me you guys are getting more serious? It's about time!"

Tara couldn't help but laugh at her friend's hopeful expression. She wanted Evan to be more serious too. They'd been friends forever, and somewhere along the way she started to fall for him. Some days she thought he felt the same, others she couldn't tell.

"Well, no, it's not that exactly," Tara said. She swallowed and felt her heart hammering. What she wanted to ask was for the time off to be on the reality television show and to spend an entire glorious month with Evan, doing something she'd always dreamed of. But how could she do that? Reality sunk in and her shoulders slumped. What company would just let someone leave for a month? Was she going to have to give her notice?

It was a really tough choice thinking about choosing between something that sounded incredible and amazing while being with Evan, and staying, working at the job she had put so much effort into that paid her bills and put a roof over her head.

Tara took a moment to try and organize her thoughts and then glanced up at Lindsay who was staring at her with a look of concern.

"If something's wrong, you can tell me," Lindsay said.

Tara bit her lip. "It's just I have a really big favor to ask and I don't want to put you on the spot because you're both my best friend and my boss and I don't want there to be some sort of weird conflict of interest thing that makes you uncomfortable."

Lindsay smiled broadly at her. "And that's why you're not only my best friend but a fantastic employee," she said. Her voice softened then, "But I'm not going to know what it is you want to ask me unless you tell me. So just say it. I'm not going to get mad at you."

Tara nodded. "Okay, a while back Evan and I were hanging out at the mall. These people were doing auditions for a reality television show, and we thought why not?"

"Oh, I think you mentioned something about that," Lindsay said. Her eyes got big. "Wait a minute! Don't tell me! Did you guys get chosen to be on it?" She leaned forward in excitement. "What's the prize? Is it like a million dollars or something you have to fight your way through a jungle to get? Your own private island you could win? Or a house in the Caribbean filled with cute singles you get to date?"

Tara laughed while she shook her head. She was glad her friend was so excited for her. "No, it's none of those things," she said. "But it is something pretty exciting to me. We did get chosen and the filming lasts for about a month. It takes place in Pennsylvania and the four of us would be living as though we were in the 1800s. But then that leads to the problem of my needing to take off of work."

Lindsay leaned back and gave a slow nod. "Say no more. I understand," she said and opened her laptop and started tapping on the keys. Tara wasn't sure what she was doing and she didn't want to ask. Lindsay was a lot of great things, but she was also kind of irritated when someone interrupted her when she was thinking.

About a minute later, Lindsay looked up at her again, her expression serious. "Okay," she said. "What are the dates?"

Tara pulled up the email on her phone and skimmed through until she found it. "The morning of July eighth is when I'm supposed to get there for outfitting and rules. We start filming that afternoon. We'll be filmed for four weeks, then on the twenty-ninth day, they tell us if we won."

With a quick nod, Lindsay turned her laptop around and sat next to Tara on the opposite side of the desk in the other vacant chair. "You have two and a half weeks of paid vacation time," she said, pointing at the screen. "I'm willing to authorize one additional week of unpaid vacation time as a one-time performance bonus for the sales you made. That just leaves the problem of three days we need to figure out. I have to be fair to the others."

Tara squeezed her best friend's hand. "Does that mean I can go?" she asked.

"Well, it means you're going to have to figure out a way to get approval for those three days, or else come back early if they don't let you go late. I can't really give you any more unaccounted for time, even if I really wanted to. There is a company to run and you have a large role in it."

"I understand," Tara said, biting her lip in thought. "There's got to be a way."

Lindsay tapped a perfectly manicured fingernail on her laptop. "Let's keep thinking," she said. They were both silent for a moment, then Lindsay said, "I don't want to suggest lying, but do you have any sick days saved up?" she asked, resuming her tapping on the computer.

"I do, Tara said. "Six days because I've not had to use them this last year."

"Perfect. That's your three days then," Lindsay said, satisfaction in her tone, "because mental health falls under a sick day request and I really can't think of anything more mentally healing for you than getting back to nature and living in your own little prairie house for a month. Once you get there, have to pee in the woods or a smelly little outhouse covered in spiders, you'll see how great it is here, and come rushing back with open arms."

Tara squealed, "You are the best friend and the best boss ever!"

Lindsey rolled her eyes and said, "Just don't let that get around. I don't want people thinking that I was playing favorites."

"I definitely won't," Tara assured her.

"Message me while you are gone," Lindsay said. "I want to know how it's going."

"If I can I will, but I assume they're not going to let us have any electronics or any communication devices except for in an emergency." Tara gave an apologetic shrug.

"Oh yeah, that's right," Lindsay said. "You'll be living in the stone age. I don't know...you're a better woman than me. I couldn't go a day without internet, let alone a month."

Tara rolled her eyes. "You've just never tried. I like unplugging on the weekend. I wish I could do it for more than a few hours, but there's always a work emergency. I really am excited. Even if I do have to use an outhouse."

"It sounds like a dream come true for you," Lindsay said. Then, she searched her friend's face. "Just promise me you're not going to have so much fun that you won't want to come back."

"No chance of that," Tara said. "I love working here with you."

"Even though you called it soul sucking?" Lindsay asked, one eyebrow arched.

"Yeah," Tara said. "But I'm hoping to come back with a huge cash prize, having had a relaxing vacation, and maybe use the time to think about my future and what I want out of it."

"And maybe get a serious boyfriend?" Lindsay teased.

Tara didn't answer, she just grinned as she waved and left her friend's office. She did have to get back. As she made her way back to her own desk, a little niggle of a worry wrapped itself in her mind. Sometimes hardships drove people apart, and living like in the 1800s was sure to have a few difficulties.

This really might be the perfect time to get closer to Evan without any distractions. They'd been friends a really long time and she wanted more. But would he be willing to take the next step in their relationship? Or was this going to be an on camera disaster waiting to happen?

NOTE FROM AUTHOR

Thank you for taking the time to read The 1800s
Experiment, Jill and Mark!
Could I ask for one small favor? Reviews like yours on
Amazon mean so much to me and help others to find my
books! Even just a single line means a lot!
Want a FREE book?
Stop by my website to get your no strings attached **FREE
book**. It's my gift to you, as a thank you for reading this
book.
www.sarahlambbooks.com

ABOUT THE AUTHOR

Sarah Lamb is the mother of two boys and wife to a teacher. She spends her days writing historical romance in the beautiful Shenandoah Valley.

WANT MORE OF SARAH'S BOOKS?

Find them all on Amazon!
https://www.amazon.com/stores/Sarah-Lamb/auth
or/B098H3SGLK